Children of the Zagros

Children of the Zagros

Shad Raouf Qazaz

Children of the Zagros

Author: Shad Raouf Qazaz

Cover Design: Julian Brzozowski
Cover Adaptation: Whitespace Agency

Adventure Novel, Magical Realism
ISBN: 979-8-90148-576-7

For all who wander,
estranged from their source,
may this offer of the heart light your way home.

Content

I
Martyr

1

What is an end, if not a beginning? It is only when the events that shape us reach their conclusion that we begin to see the story which led us here. As such, every beginning is also a farewell to a part of ourselves, with pain or relief, with anxiety or respite, it is always a being born anew.

It is at that moment where the old passes into the new, where the end is fertile with the beginning, when our princess retreats and closes herself off from the rest of the royal family.

The royal couple had three male heirs to succeed them. Each of them were talented men, gifted with all the qualities that a head of state should possess. But in the safety of their marital bed, the choice fell on their youngest daughter.

It was the queen who first saw the young princess' insistent look, even on the first day she weaned the child. 'She looked at me with the most vivid eyes,' she had said to her husband. An insight that fell on deaf ears.

Only when the years passed by, did the king also notice that extraordinary clarity of his daughter. And it took him another few years before he could see what his queen already had felt. She lay in bed when he entered and woke her with a kiss. 'Gelawezj, your intuition has always been years ahead of mine,' he whispered, harkening back to a conversation that had been evaded all that time, but one which the queen knew would someday come.

'You've always needed time to feel what you already know,' she said with half-closed eyes.

The king caressed her graying hair as he sat next to her on the bed. In all those years her beauty had only grown, as if her soul's beauty shone through the wrinkles on her face. They looked at each other with the same love as in their younger years, a rare moment of tenderness in their present lives.

His face became earnest. 'But we have three older sons, each enjoying more popularity and showing more talent.'

Gelawezj lay still. 'That's correct.'

'And to pass them over, that would be a grave breach of tradition.'

The queen opened her eyes, and her expression hardened. 'Sherwan. You are king. Not your father and not his father. You.'

The young princess did not have the charisma of her brothers, who were loved by all the people. The sons would miss no opportunity to drum up the most beautiful stories and whip up the people's pride and emotions. And with their generous character, they earned the loyalty of those same people.

The princess also did not possess knowledge of history and statecraft, knowledge that her brothers had learned from the best teachers in the land. Nor had she proven her qualities as a leader by leading troops to victory or her courage by charging into battle as head of an army. Despite her disinterest in learning the proper customs and her unwillingness to acquire the knowledge required of a head of state, the king now realized that she was the only one who could provide his subjects with the care needed to lead their people's history out of the darkness.

A long time ago, their ancestors had left the darkness of Shaneder behind them. None of the living knew the fear of residing in that cave. Despite the fissure, the darkness had seeped into their hearts and followed them from generation to generation. No matter how far they moved and how many city walls they built, in times of silence it banged on the door of their consciousness, as an unexpected guest or plunderer. Which of the two it was, no one knew, for no one dared to answer, preferring the warmth of their hearth over the unknown darkness outside.

The young princess would cut through that darkness and usher in a new age. She would cast into the light what stalked them and free them from this burdensome past. It was a small spark the king dared to embrace, fueled by the support and encouragement of the queen. He dared to be brave and, against his viziers' counsel and the people's expectations, follow his heart as if he were a free man.

Their ancestors had been abandoned in Shaneder as children, set in the Zagros Mountains. None of them knew why they were there or what was expected of them. In that cave, they learned how to survive on the little bits of food that were brought in by a new child each day; every day another child that did not know where they had ended up, let alone why. The daily rations were added to by what they could scavenge together in their surroundings. Too fearful to explore the unknown world, they remained close to their cave. Only the brave and the naïve dared to venture into fields further away, to return with what little extras could be foraged. It happened all too often that they did not return at all. The men that brought them here had warned them that any attempt to run would result in a certain death. And so, the threat of death, by man or nature, was a constant factor in their lives.

Until one day, a child arrived with more than just rations; they carried a closed box with them. The children had gotten used to the rhythm of their days in which they did little more than have conversations, take care of food, invent new games, and wait for the next day. This new and unexpected element caused discord in their midst. Many approached the box with suspicion. That the child did not know what was inside only increased that suspicion. They decided to throw the box in a deep hole where no one could reach it. Unless they had the courage to jump in the dark and brave the chilling rattling of snakes.

The next day, no new child arrived and the days after neither. The routine they had become accustomed to was upended without any warning. In all that time, they had not wondered whether they should leave. That answer was carved into their limbs by the warnings of their kidnappers. But now discussions erupted again about what they should do. One group was convinced that the lack of any new children was a sign of the downfall of their kidnappers, so they should try to find their way home. Another group was not convinced and preferred the safety of their new environment instead of returning to a place that seemed more like a distant nightmare than a home.

The discussion heavily raged on, as more children took on a passive role. They conformed to those that either seemed to show more courage or seemed to stand starkly behind their conviction. In this first true discussion that they ever had, the seeds were sown for their eventual hierarchy. They were too young when kidnapped to have been aware of customs and habits. But they knew that some people obeyed others. And they knew that those that obeyed were not as convinced of themselves as those that were were being obeyed. So many conformed to those that spoke with conviction about what they could achieve by leaving their cave.

And thus, they left, for the first time, the safe environment they had learned to know. They settled on the mountainside of

Bradost, one of many peaks in the Zagros Mountains. The few that were most acquainted with their surroundings, because they had dared to explore them, were also the ones that appropriated the role of shepherd, a role that the fearful among them happily passed over. And slowly, growing throughout generations, their settlements became villages, and they explored more areas and even reached the plateaus below the mountain to finally raise a first city, and generations later, a kingdom.

During their expansions, they discovered multiple groups of children, whose origins were the same as theirs. The first encounters were weary and full of uncertainty. With the passage of time the groups became larger and more organized, and uncertainty gained a companion: suspicion. Conflicts arose and ranks were set, until the hierarchies between the groups became a reflection of the stability within them.

The settlements became larger, and the population grew. The more this went on, the more the people looked to their local leaders for protection. Consequently, their informal roles slowly became a matter of course and rulers took measures to maintain power within their family by having their children succeed them.

One day they awoke and had forgotten those were mere roles, and the old dynamics of king and subject, parent and child, strong and weak, once again crystallized as the norm. The rift with their past and the docile attitude that many had taken determined the structures of their society, akin to how dunes of the desert determine the caravans' routes. The people were content to lead their lives as shepherds, merchants, farmers, or see to their livelihood in another way, knowing that a great danger at any moment could return to rip them away from the safety of their loved ones.

It was this history of their bloodline the king had received from his grandfather on the day they visited the primordial cave of his people. The dynasty that had appropriated the role of shepherd and later of kings, had also passed on their insights from generation to generation. So that each new king could better protect them from the danger that remained unknown. But just as his grandfather had instructed him, each generation made the mistake of hiding from the darkness, keeping it at bay with games and pleasure, with hard work and songs. No one possessed the inner awareness to face that darkness, to bring about reconciliation with the past, and thus, for the first time, to rejoice as a people in a future that would welcome them with a smile.

The king had searched his whole life for a way to bring his grandfather's wisdom to reality. Now that his face resembled his grandfather's, it dawned on him that he would not be able to complete the task with which he was burdened. His life had logged on the necessary maintenance of a kingdom; enacting war to remain in power, ruling over judicial matters, politicking to prevent wars – and to remain in power.

Even now, in times of peace, the hours of the day escaped him so quickly that his mission had not advanced even one step. Every time there was a new obstacle that demanded his immediate attention, but the princess was like a beacon of light that drove away the darkness. She was the hope he had searched for and to whom he could entrust the future. So, despite the expectations for his oldest son to rise to the throne, he chose, thanks to the attentiveness and encouragement of his queen, his daughter as his heir. The viziers followed his determination and the people, cautious but full of trust, rested in the knowledge that their king was wise and noble. That was enough for them to accept the diversion from tradition.

It was shortly after their announcement that the princess retreated to her wing of the palace. All her maids were sent away and for days no one heard from her. The door to her wing remained closed. None of the keys worked and requests to open it remained unanswered.

2

At first, they thought it was a fit, an understandable emotional reaction for her age. The safety of the princess was not in doubt, but the absence of a public appearance would endanger the supposed stability of the royal house and stagger the people's trust, two fundamental pillars of their kingdom. The king would be blamed for deviating from tradition and bringing disaster upon himself. This would imply that he was no longer able to protect them, the foundational pillar of his authority.

In an effort to resolve the situation quickly and indoors, he enlisted the help of two respected men: a magician and an architect. The architect would search for structural weaknesses in the door and the magician could find any spiritual blockades and dispel them. Both men were escorted through the palace by the king's personal guard, the warrior Akam.

A double door, engraved with the symbol of the royal house, the red-legged partridge, marked the entrance to the princess' wing. The small bird, drawn the size of a human, had a red beak that blended into the white of its neck. Its head was rimmed by a black line that began around its eyes and ended at the bottom of its neck. Its ash blue blended into maroon on its back and wings. Its chest was grey and red stripes on its sides pointed toward its red feet in the same color as its beak.

The architect started investigating the double door with his tools. The magician rustled through his bags, took out various herbs and mixed these in a bowl.

The architect looked studiously at the corners of the door and banged with a hammer on a few spots. 'Do you know who made these doors?' he asked their escort.

'I do not, sir. I would need to ask around to find the answer.' Akam stood with his spear in hand like a watcher.

'How were they brought here?'

'The doors were already here before my enlistment. I would have to inquire with...'

'What about the temperature swings between summer and winter?' The architect hit another few spots on the door with a chisel.

Akam did not understand what the architect was getting at. 'I am not aware of...'

'Does water leak inside when it pours?'

Akam gripped his spear. The questions were getting on his nerves, and he became impatient due to the lack of action. How were the weather and herbs supposed to make the door open? Before he could answer, they were distracted by the scent of burning herbs.

The architect made space for the magician, who placed his bowl in front of the door. He laid multiple plants around it in a circle. The ingredients in the bowl produced enough smoke to obscure the door until the partridge seemed to dance to the rhythm of the smoke.

The magician joined the other two. 'If a djinn closed that door with magic, we will smoke him out with this.'

Finally, something we can work with, the warrior thought. But no matter how much smoke rose up and how pungent the scent of the herbs became, no djinn came out.

The magician and architect started discussing their techniques, hoping to find a way out of the impasse by an exchange of ideas. This moment of reflection agitated their impatient escort even more. He did not understand why so much caution needed to be displayed for a door, while the princess might be in danger. Thoughts curled around in his body until they became stronger than his instructions. His body moved as if by itself and he stormed towards the door. With the small round shield on his arm, he rammed through the doors in one bash.

The other two were so engulfed in their conversation that it was not until they heard the bang that they noticed that Akam was no longer next to them. They had to wait until the smoke and dust lifted to see the door was broken open and he was wiping off debris on the other side.

Astonished, but also relieved that the door was not broken by them, they walked into the hallway. A hallway where servants used to diligently walk back and forth to meet the princess' every need. Now a deathly silence ruled.

None of the rooms they inspected showed any signs of destruction or robbery, but the princess was also nowhere to be found. It was as if, since the servants had left, everything had remained exactly as it was, without even a speck of dust having settled.

Arriving at the door that led to the princess' bedroom, the three men were extra careful. They aimed their eyes at the ground when opening, to prevent them from seeing the princess at an improper moment or create the impression their intentions were less than honorable.

The foot end of the princess' bed was the first thing they saw. Next to that a pair of legs. A woman stood as a watcher next to the princess' bed. 'Welcome, gentlemen. You may enter. The princess awaits you.'

The men walked into the room. A linen canopy hung around the bed, showing a sitting silhouette.

'Princess!' the magician exclaimed. 'Thank God you are safe. We are here to get you out. I am sure you could use some fresh air.'

'Only one of you will get me out.' A soft girl's voice sounded inside the canopy.

The canopy opened and the men aimed their eyes at the ground. The princess sat cross-legged on the bed. The light shone on her porcelain face, that was kept safe from the darkening many endured by their daily toil under the hot sun. Her smooth skin had a subtle glow. Her black hair rested on her shoulders and her small pupils were lined by dark irises.

She bent forward and took in her so-called saviors. The men felt her eyes, as if her growing pupils were trying to penetrate them. She saw one of them was covered in wood chips and dust. 'Did you smash my door, master Akam?'

The warrior bent over under the weight of the realization that the princess was displeased with him. 'My deepest apologies, princess. I broke open the doors. I wanted to prevent you from having to wait any longer in case you were in danger. My actions were hasty and thoughtless. I will pay for all the repairs myself.'

The princess watched him apologize patiently. 'My double doors were a work of art by a master artist. Don't you know art can never be repaired, as it is a unique expression of the artist's soul?

The warrior turned red, consumed by shame. 'You are right, princess. I have made my actions worse with my callous choice of words.'

'But it is exactly such audacity that I need!' she exclaimed unexpectedly.

Akam sprang up at the princess' call.

'Today is the day I leave the palace and venture out into the world. And to accompany me on such a journey, a protector of stature is needed – one who will shrink from neither symbols nor men.'

The other two men suppressed their laughter.

The architect walked towards the princess. 'Come now, little princess. We can't make your parents wait any longer. Everyone's worrie...'

The man flew against the wall, led by the hand of the woman next to the bed.

'Keep an appropriate distance, gentlemen, as well in the room as in your choice of words.'

The magician stood still. 'The world is a dangerous place, princess. Full of roving gangs, beasts! And what of the enemies of your father?

The princess rolled her eyes but did not answer. Her attention was on Akam.

He was quiet. As soon as the princess had made her demand, he felt the strength of her will. First in her voice and then in the determination of her gaze. It was a self-confidence he only had experienced in her father and now she, as his heir, was asking him to go against the will of the king. By taking the young heiress from the palace, his death would be assured. That he was only fulfilling the princess' wish, would drown in the retribution for his betrayal. Despite this knowledge a will stirred within him, not quite his nor alien to him, that urged him to forget the dangers of the future and promises of the past and honor this child's wish.

Once again, his body moved on its own before his thoughts could reach a conclusion. 'Climb on my back, princess.'

She reacted with childish enthusiasm. 'Amazing!'

The princess stepped off the bed and did as he asked. They jumped straight down through the window on the second floor and Akam landed in the gardens with ease.

He had made his way to the stables and placed the princess on the horse before anyone had investigated the shattering of windows. His horse, Raksh, neighed as he recognized his master and again to welcome his guest.

Like the wind, they rode to the city gates. Raksh' long strides were recognized from a distance by the guards and the city gates remained open to allow the famed hero and his stallion passage. The princess sat in front of him, concealed under his cloak.

Once they passed the city gates, she showed herself. 'Tonight, we follow the Zab, Akam. The river.

'Yes, princess.'

'But before we do that, you must say goodbye to your wife.'

'I must advise against that, princess. As soon as they find out what happened at the palace, that will be the first place they search for us.'

'This goodbye cannot be skipped. It must happen.' The princess was resolute, her voice full of authority.

Akam remained silent and obeyed her command. He fought the relief he felt at being allowed to see his wife and daughter. He fought against the softening of his heart in the light of his duty; it did not behoove him to place his desires above the safety of his princess. Yet, he could not resist looking forward to the warmth of his home at the edge of the forest. He tightened the reins and urged Raksh to quicken his pace.

3

The sun had begun its descent when they arrived at Akam's home. A woman with long blond curls awaited them. A daughter stood up from her games at the sound of hoofs. She called for her father as soon as Raksh came into sight and her mother picked her up. The woman's eyes softened momentarily before they fell upon the passenger atop the horse. Akam fastened his horse on a pole and walked toward them.

The princess had ordered Akam to go inside alone.

He nearly fell off his horse hearing those words. 'Princess, it is much too dangerous to leave you outside. On top of that, my wife would never forgive me for not hosting you as a guest in our home.'

The princess held Raksh's mane softly to stay in balance. 'It's unbecoming for a stranger to be in your home at this moment. You are saying goodbye to the mother of your child and that must happen in the safety of your relationship. My presence would add too many formalities to that moment, and formalities are the deathblow of longing hearts.'

The princess caressed Raksh' manes as she watched how Akam embraced his family. His shield and sword could safely be undone here and his love had space to radiate. After the happiness of reuniting, a shadow of seriousness fell over the lovers. Slowly it dawned on his wife who the person sitting on Raksh was. The sweet surprise of Akam's return came with a bitter aftertaste.

'Let's go inside, Hanar. I will explain.'

The princess stayed behind on the field, accompanied by a grazing Raksh. She inhaled deeply and took in the fresh air of the forest, a vastly different air than those of the walls and carpets in the palace. The rippling of the river carried her thoughts so that there was nothing else at that moment other than the fresh air and the creak. The sun colored the sky from deep red to baby blue and the first stars showed themselves. She enjoyed the blue on her skin, the green of life around her and the warmth of the light of the house.

With a deep sigh she exhaled her life of royalty and made space for something new, something unknown.

When Akam and Hanar stepped outside, the sky had completely transformed into a dark blue. Under the stars, the two lovers looked at each other and Akam saw in his wife's eyes the same happenings of years past, when their love was still budding and he handled her heart with careless disregard.

On that day, years ago, he witnessed how the space between them stretched out in an instant to an unbridgeable distance, deep as the ocean and harsh as the tundra. Her heart retreated to a fort that was built on events from long before he knew her. That fort protected her against the dangers outside with walls of apathy. In the dusk of the light in her eyes, he saw her locked-away heart. He also saw the power needed to suppress such an overwhelming love. It filled him with an awe that made the fire within him burn with the intensity of a warm hearth on a dark winter night.

His life as a warrior had been shaped by bloody battles and grueling marches. His movements, thoughts, and fighting were the result of a determination to protect what was worth protecting. His warrior's heart, though, wasn't formed until the spiritual trek to his lover's heart, a heart that beat in the same rhythm as his, a rhythm formed long before their birth, with the same brush strokes as the starry sky above them.

He trod inside. He did not know if it was inside him or her, but he kept on going. He withstood sea storms and kept the flame burning across the chilling tundra. The love in her heart must shine its light. Even she herself would not deprive the world of it. Forsaking himself and ignoring her rejections, he traversed deeper until one day he reached the walls of the fort. He did not knock, for there were no doors. He did not attack, for it was impregnable. He did not yell, for no sound could penetrate the fortress.

The only sign of life was the beating of her heart that shook the walls from the inside, a pounding that screamed for release. The shockwaves traveled across the tundra and created the ocean waves he had narrowly survived. That same throbbing had been his compass during the travels through his inner most fears and those of hers. And here they were so strong that merely standing straight was a struggle.

Knowing that no plea, request, or attack would have any effect, he did the only thing remaining. He reached into his chest and tore it open, so that his heart could go freely to what it desired. He allowed it to go outside his body and guided it with every beat to the fort. The walls melted into a nourishing nectar and covered the tundra. The dry ground slowly turned into an oasis of flora and fauna. The light of her heart shined in all the land and her glow bathed him in a love that nourished every cell.

Where his heart beat earlier in his chest, only the fire that was awakened in him remained. He did not miss his heart because he knew it was safe with her. There was no more loving caretaker. Just as her love wasn't hers to hide, his heart wasn't his to keep.

Today, both relived those events once more. It was only when he felt both hearts beating in unison that Akam turned around and walked to the princess. He wore beige harem pants, held up with a dark green sash. On top is a red vest lined with golden accents. On his side hung his scimitar and a spear with a red pom behind the blade rested against his shoulder. His sun-brown skin had more grooves than others of his age. In the little light left, his thick brows cast a shadow over his brown eyes. With his pointed beard, his face looked like a shadow from a distance.

The princess waited for him where he had left her: on his trusty steed, Raksh. He hopped on, with the princess in front of him and rode towards the bush. A pressing silence, one even the princess didn't talk through, accompanied the two travelers.

Once enclosed by the forest, Akam broke the silence. 'What is our destination, princess?'

'For now, only the Zab,' she replied.

'What are we looking for exactly, princess?' His face remained fixed on the forest path in front of them.

The princess saw only his beard. 'That's an important question, Akam. What is any one of us looking for? What are you looking for? It's a question we should ask ourselves more often.'

'I'm only here to serve you, princess. Aside from your safety and accomplishing your wishes, there is no other goal for me.' His voice sounded dutiful but distant, as if a part of him remained with his wife.

Behind them the full moon shone through the vegetation. The light occasionally caught the eyes of the animals who called the forest home.

'That is honorable, Akam the warrior,' the princess answered in recognition. 'A servant's goal is always clearer than a ruler's. He can't set any wrong goals. The only thing he needs to worry about is obeying with diligence. In contrast, a leader can set their sights on anything and in that freedom, she runs the risk of aspiring to foolish or devilish goals.'

'God forbid that you would ever be roped in by the devil, princess!'

A second silence followed, which was filled up by the sound of Rakhs' hooves, the soft babbling water, and the rustling of wind in the leaves.

'I don't know what our goal is, Akam, or what it is that we are searching for. I know only the path we must take and for now that is next to this water. The water will lead us where we need to be.'

When Raksh' panting became heavier and Akam's sharpness faded, it was time to rest. They searched for a sheltered spot to set up camp. For the first time in her life, the princess lay in the outdoor air. The scent of the ground and humid air tickled her senses. The wind now and then revealed parts of the moon as the trees swerved. Enjoying this play between heaven and earth, she fell asleep, thinking of the story her mother had told her once about the moon's inception.

The queen smiled as if something inside her was being tickled – a memory from long ago, one she had forgotten even existed. 'My beautiful flower, the moon was once a girl, almost as pretty as you, that shone like light. Her name was Heyv. One day her mother was kneading dough to make bread. She mixed flour, water, yeast, and salt to eventually form a thin circle and baked it against the side of the stone clay oven.'

'An oven like we have here?' the princess, who had just mastered speaking, asked.

'Even better than the ovens we have here! But soon the mother realized that the dough would be too dry. You know how dry bread tastes, right, sweetheart?'

'Yes, Yuck! When it's a day old.'

'Right!'

'And I never want to eat that, but you make me, mommy. I want the good bread.'

The queen smiled again. Her daughter's pure desires filled her with warmth from inside. 'Yes, yes, I know, little one. But we're talking about the moon now, not your eating habits.'

The princess pursed her lips in protest.

'So,' her mother said while petting her. 'There was no water left, so the mother sent her daughter to the local spring to fetch water.'

'Mommy, what's a spring?'

'Ah! A spring is a place where the clearest water sprouts directly from the mountain. See Korek Mountain, there outside your window? It has many springs from which the purest and coldest water flows without stopping. Even people on long journeys can count on the Zagros' generosity. And during picnics there's always a creek to keep the fruit cool.'

The small princess' eyes widened. 'Wow!' Her amazement quickly turned into confusion. 'But why isn't the mountain wet?'

The mother, surprised by the question, burst into laughter. 'Maybe one day you can find out for yourself? But let's not forget about Heyv.'

'The pretty girl!

'Right. So pretty that even during her walk to the spring, she was stared at by everyone. Everyone wanted to stop her and have a chance to speak with her. She was so beautiful that no one could just let her pass. Because everyone wanted to share a word with her, she returned very late. Her mother had been waiting all that time with the dry dough in her hands. She was so angry that she slapped her daughter with those doughy hands.'

The queen demonstrated where Heyv was hit by rubbing her daughter's face. 'The dough stuck to Heyv's face, and she ran away crying. In her sadness she prayed to be taken away from that place. And before her mother's eyes, Heyv's pleas were answered and she rose up to transform into the moon. That's why the moon is full of spots. That's the dough.'

4

Early in the morning the princess saw a clove apple floating in the river. 'Akam, look!'

Akam was saddling Raksh when the princess called him. He hurried towards her. 'What's the matter, princess?'

She gleefully pointed at the river. 'a clove apple. Lovers are nearby.'

'I'm surprised you know what purpose it serves, princess. Nowadays it's a custom only found in small villages.'

The princess was squatting at the river, trying to grab the apple, but it was just outside her reach. 'Did you also fill an apple with cloves as a gift to Hanar?'

Akam looked around. 'No, it's more something for young girls to express their feelings in a proper manner.' He saw a figure squatting close to the river a bit further off. 'Princess, someone's there. Remain seated,' he whispered.

The princess immediately rose up and waved at the figure. 'Why did you drop your apple in the river? Don't you know it keeps longer if dried? What will your beloved say when she discovers you lost her present? Or are you in love with the water?'

Up close they saw it was a boy, of about the princess' age. His red eyes and the fresh tears that washed away the dirt from his face made him a sad sight to behold.

He answered with a broken voice. 'My beloved is no longer on this earth. The most precious thing she gave me, I now give back to the water so that it will not go to waste when I take my revenge.'

'And who will you be taking your revenge on, if I may ask?' the princess asked with piqued interest.

The boy looked up and sadness made room for anger. 'The king.'

Akam's sword had almost left its sheath before the boy finished, ready to end his adventure. 'No, Akam!' the princess shouted. 'I want to know what's the matter with this boy. Why are you planning to take revenge on the king?'

He wiped the tears from his face. 'Because it's his fault that my beloved is dead. We had known each other since we were small and each day we played together. But from the moment I began herding the sheep daily and she took care of housekeeping, we were forbidden to play together. I missed her dearly and she must have felt the same, because one day I saw her out in the field. There, away from prying eyes, our feelings finally blossomed, and I dared to hold her hand, like I had done so often. But this time it was different. In the weeks that followed, she found a way to meet me in the field almost daily and each day we discovered more of the pleasures of each other's bodies.

But her parents discovered our escapades and turned into beasts. They dragged her through the street by her hair, and one by one her brothers, cousins and uncles took as many stones to hand as possible until she lay lifeless on the ground, covered in blood and dirt.'

Akam's thoughts wandered off to his wife. The idea of a life without her offered him the chance to feel the boy's pain. He did not permit himself to ponder what he would do if that had been his daughter.

The princess had never experienced such love but understood the boy was feeling a great sorrow. 'Still, the situation could have been solved if you had wed her,' she said.

'They didn't give me the chance!' he shouted. 'We wanted nothing more than to share our life together. But as soon as they found out, they piled on her like deranged beasts, as if with stones and her blood they could recover their honor!'

The princess was impressed by the boy's raw emotions. She was curious how far he was prepared to go. 'And what do you expect from the king? Her family has taken care of the matter, and they even still have something owed to them by you.'

'What kind of king would accept this!?'

Akam buried his elbow in the boy's sniffling nose. 'Watch your words, boy.'

He fell to his knees and caught blood from his nose with his hand. 'They said they were only following the king's laws, but when I asked which ones, they couldn't answer me. When I escaped, I swore to find the king and find out what he thinks of this for myself.'

'And what if the king doesn't agree with you?' the princess asked.

'Then I'll bring him to ruin myself and destroy the privilege of those beasts who distort love so heinously.'

Akam gripped the handle of his sword and looked back for permission. The princess didn't have the same reverence for the king as her protector, nor his need for honor. The swirling storm of anger, sorrow, despair, and arrogance was a spectacle for her, which she enjoyed.

'Akam, give our avenger a hand. You've needlessly hurt this harmless boy. And offer him something to eat. He will need it on his quest.'

Akam sighed the tension of readiness away. He had gotten used to the princess' firm decisions by now.

The boy hoggishly began eating. His tears once again began to flow as he sobbed. The anger churned in his mind, and he turned inward. The instigators of his beloved's fate clumped together until he only saw himself as her true murderer. Soon, the cursing of his neighbors slowly morphed into a cursing of himself.

He finished the food, washed his hands and face clean in the river, and thanked the two for their generosity. He introduced himself as Hemin.

'Runak is my name,' the princess said.

Hemin smiled. 'Just like the princess!'

'That's right,' Runak said, as she answered his smile. 'Just like the princess.'

The girl across from him reminded Hemin of his beloved. They didn't look alike, but Runak's smile radiated the same warmth as the sun reflected off the face of his beloved.

They said goodbye and went on their way. Hemin went downstream and Akam and Runak, following the instructions of the boy, went to his village. 'I want to see what kind of people can kill their own daughter,' the princess proclaimed after Hemin's departure.

They found, to their surprise, a village that in no way seemed to be in crisis. The people were even elated and out and about. Women were kneading, squatting in the outside air. They threw dough in a thin layer on a saj, a convex iron plate that was heated by open fire, which transformed the dough in no time into naan bread.

A shepherd pushed his cattle toward his home. He was using his walking stick to whip up the animals when he saw the new arrivals. 'Welcome, good sir and young lady.'

'Thank you, good man. Can you tell us why it is so lively here today?' Akam asked.

The shepherd lit up. 'Our precious cousin Rebin has returned. You look tired. Tonight, you will be our guests!'

'That is very kind,' Akam answered, 'but we don't want to bother you.'

'None of that! Our pir's diwan, the village elder, is free and always available for travelers such as yourself.' He gestured for them to follow him.

'Akam, what is a diwan?' the princess asked.

'The diwan is where the pir hosts meetings and houses guests. There they discuss the village's most important matters.'

The princess thought for a moment. 'Kind of like a court?'

Akam looked back at the princess. She was sitting on Raksh. 'Right. At court they also discuss important matters.'

Runak shook her head. 'No, not because of that.'

'Because of what, then, princess?'

'Because here too, one day they sentence someone to death and celebrate the next.'

After the evening meal, Akam, the princess, the returned cousin Rebin, the village elder, and many villagers gathered in the diwan. They sat upon colorful carpets on the ground and supported themselves with just as colorful pillows. The company sat against the walls of the diwan and in the middle, women and young children walked back and forth with canisters of water, trays of sunflower seeds and nuts, and tea glasses. Lively conversations filled the room and the streets around the diwan. They laughed and chatted, some joked amongst themselves, and others played games with large hand gestures.

The noise in the room slowly died down and the pir took the word. 'Dear family members and dear friends. Today, finally, our traveler, our explorer, has returned. The man who has seen the whole world and still prefers his own small village, Rebin!'

'Long live that brave boy!' An echo of the people strengthening the pir's words resounded.

The pir gestured with his hands and calmed the group. 'Tell us, Rebin. Of all the people you have seen and met, which were the most noteworthy?'

The young man stroked his red beard. 'A beautiful question, indeed.' He directed his gaze to the group. 'Brothers and sisters, I have traveled beyond the protection of the Zagros to places with strange scents and even stranger tastes. Places where they had buildings with red round roofs, where they were able to transport water across kilometers, sometimes via channels made of stone, meters above the ground, and where their people had a different color skin than us. But what I remember most is a small kingdom far in the west. They live there in a city built entirely from a beautiful stone called marble. They make statues that are lifelike – no, even more lifelike than real people. They live in a temperate climate, not like us, scorching hot in the summer and freezing in winter. Life there is kind to them.'

'Okay, but do they also have girls?' a voice said from amongst the guests.

'You just worry about not losing your sheep before trying to find a wife,' another said, followed by laughter.

Rebin continued after the laughter died down. 'And because maintenance of life doesn't require much, everyone has time to meddle in the decisions of their city. To prevent total chaos from breaking out, they have devised the following. After a brief discussion they will list the different options one by one. Everyone puts up their hand when their preferred option is called and the option with the most hands is selected.'

A haze of confusion spread through the diwan. The listeners began murmuring amongst each other, each turning to their neighbor to be sure of what they just heard.

'So, what most people want is what they then do?' a confused attendee asked.

'That's right! They call it voting and the votes ultimately decide.'

Once again, the murmuring returned. People spoke up in disbelief and occasional laughter broke out. 'Everyone who wants to do nothing and just sleep tomorrow, put your hands in the air!' one of the voices sounded. Laughing, everyone put up their hand. 'And why can't the sheep vote on when they get shaved?' They surpassed each other, each with ever more crazy suggestions that were received with growing enthusiasm.

In the commotion Runak turned to Akam. 'I know what our destination is,' she whispered through the commotion. 'Ask him later what the way to this kingdom is.'

'As you wish...' He looked around to reassure himself his neighbor was in conversation, '...princess.'

The pir once again calmed the group. 'How is it possible then that they built such grand buildings and gathered wisdom if they merely follow the whims of the majority, dear Rebin?'

'That's simple! They have an army of slaves to do all the work, from household chores to constructing the buildings!'

'Oh, no.' The pir shook his head in dismay and looked at the attendees. 'What a loss it is for a man to not provide for his own family, or for a woman to not honor her husband when he returns home, or for the children to not help their parents in this same distribution. My dear fellow villagers, let no spectacle of written words and grand buildings distract you from the bliss of a righteous life, lived in respect for your superiors and care for your kin. Take this lesson and hold it close to your hearts and that is to always, in each environment, in the family, in the community, and in a kingdom consult your elder and accept their wisdom.'

Agreeable noises filled the room.

'Even if it's a woman?' a soft voice said. The young girl, with a tea tray in her hands, seemed surprised herself that her thoughts had turned into words. Her mother pulled her arm to silence her.

'Let the girl ask questions,' the pir said. 'That's how children learn. Child, the wise Lord has given man and woman each their own domain. And because the man is naturally less subject to emotions and takes to the outside world, it is his responsibility to provide for the family. But he also has limits. I would, for example, never tell my wife how to cook rice. Hahaha.'

The group shared in the elder's laughter.

'Is that all women are good for? Cooking rice?' The girl was not finished. The mother's hand wrapped tighter around the small wrist and tried to force her to sit. But the girl only became more steadfast.

The elder recovered from his jovial laugh and brushed a tear away. 'But little girl, why do you think cooking rice is a futile task? Many children welcome the rice with more enthusiasm than their own father. Respect both your parents because each has their own role to fulfill, just as you one day will have a role to fulfill.'

5

The next day Akam and the princess left at dawn. They were received kindly and treated to entertaining conversations. But even so, or maybe because of it, they left with a feeling as strange as the one they arrived with. Even Akam, whose stomach churned at the thought of his daughter permitting herself such indecent adventures, could not push aside the pain in Hemin's eyes and could not exchange it for the family's honor. It would have been unbecoming for a guest to ask about the incident, and they did not see any defeated faces in the group. Except for the pent-up anger in the young girl's words who went against the pir, in this village, it seemed nothing was amiss.

The princess and the warrior made their way to Badinan. In this city they would find a guide in one of the many teahouses who could accompany them through the unknown lands to where they could cross the sea and into the land of slaves and voting, where statues seemed human and where the humans seemed to be carved out of stone. They would follow the Zab until they reached the forests of Mount Gara. Through the Gara forests they would eventually reach Badinan.

The lush green forest greeted them with a refreshing welcome. The thick vegetation sheltered them from the warm afternoon sun, and they were surrounded by life, from the insects to each waving leaf on the trees. Both were quiet, sunken in thoughts that took their own course. The images, memories, and words flowed into each other until their consciousness lost itself in Raksh' rhythmic clopping and their thoughts became a distant phenomenon.

The thick vegetation opened out into an empty field. The abrupt transition brought them back to the immediacy of their senses. In the middle of the field stood a large tree, whose branches were spread out lavishly and into a thick bush, as if they housed an unknown world of their own. Around the tree grew a colony of mushrooms. The leaves rustled in the wind and the branches moved along playfully, greeting the two guests. The massive tree's body, rooted deeply in the earth, forced the wind to maneuver around it.

The princess and Akam walked toward this centurion being. Once they passed the reach of its thrown shadow, they heard a hissing sound. A snake slithered around the tree, slowly working its way up. Black scales scraped the brown bark and left traces of the skin from its belly. Its forked tongue eagerly moved in and out to savor the scent of the chirping chicks hidden in the vegetation.

The princess became overwhelmed with pity, realizing innocent animals were about to become prey to this calculating predator. 'Akam, kill that snake and save the birds,' she whispered.

The warrior walked forward with mindful steps, making sure not to step on anything that could give away his approach. Each step was followed by a pause to assure himself he had not been spotted. He approached the tree where the tip of his sword could reach the bark and patiently paused. The snake was on the other side, unaware of what awaited it.

As soon as it reared its head, Akam sliced with a swift strike of his scimitar, dividing the snake in two, body severed from head. The animal fell lifeless into the grass as its blood mixed with the red of the mushrooms.

The princess sighed in relief.

A shadow, larger than the trees, fell over the area. Above them they heard the loud flapping of wings. They looked up and saw the contours of a gigantic bird, whose open wings reached even further than the ends of the widespread branches of the tree. The creature had wings like a peacock, of copper and green. It held on tightly to the tree, with powerful claws buried in the bark. Piercing eyes, bigger than a human head, watching them closely. The wings folded up. Even now the animal looked bigger than an elephant.

Neither of the two humans dared to move, their senses overladen with incomprehensible impressions.

Eventually the creature spoke with a female voice that seemed to echo in their thoughts. 'Worthy – warrior. You – have saved my young – from this – treacherous snake.' The rhythm with which she spoke was methodical and calculated. 'With that – you also – have saved the harvests of the World – for now until long after your death – and everything you know. What is it that I – Simurgh – responsible for cleansing of the land – and the water – mediator between heaven and earth – can bestow upon you as a reward – for this heroic feat?

Akam had been stunned from the first sight of Simurgh. His first thought was that this creature had been sent by the king's magicians to tear him to pieces. Only when Simurgh made her intentions clear could he relax. He couldn't feel anything but awe and bowed before he spoke, an expression of respect that until now had been reserved for members of the royal house. 'I am only an extension of the will of my mistress, o wise Simurgh. Responsible for all you attribute to me are her wise orders.'

The princess, also for the first time in her life, saw a bow for someone that wasn't related to her. The solemnity with which

Akam made his bow, urged her to follow suit. So, she was on equal footing with someone outside the royal family for the first time, in her honoring of a creature that surpassed her comprehension.

Simurgh took a few steps to the side. With each step she buried her claws in the bark of the tree, and from each wound she created, fresh flowers sprouted. 'This peculiar - human tendency to - make others responsible for - their deeds - has already outlived the World three times - and might even - outlive me.' Her enormous body shook the tree, and all kinds of fruits and nuts fell to the ground. 'And so also - today.' There was no judgement in her tone, only the attentiveness with which humans behold the motherly love for her cub or her brutal tearing apart a calf. 'As you wish - warrior. You are hereby - absolved of the responsibility - for your deed.'

She turned to the princess. 'What shall be your reward - princess of the young - kingdom near the Zagros?'

How does she know who I am, the princess thought. As if she had heard her think, Simurgh continued, 'all that - the light touches - falls under my domain - and with that all - knowledge of that domain.'

Due to her nobility, Runak had always seen to her needs and wishes. She had gotten used to simply taking what she wanted. But she had never experienced the openness of being asked what she wanted. From the first moment a question presented itself, but as if she didn't want to hear, it needed to repeat itself until it remained as the only option, screaming to be heard.

'What is the truth of this world?'

It was a strange question, not one Simurgh expected. She flapped her wings to order them. A gust of wind fell over the two humans.

'That answer – cannot be gifted – nor received. The truth – of this World can only – be experienced.'

'Where do I go to experience it?' the princess immediately asked.

Simurgh laughed heartily. 'Young princess – who is on the verge of learning to ask questions – your fate is as clear as the sun – but your eyes are naively set on the unknown – and therein – lies your strength and your downfall.'

Simurgh paused to observe the princess' look. She saw that the young child took in each word she uttered. And even though most of it was like an incomprehensible mist, not an answer to her questions, she didn't seem confused or disappointed. She seemed to be searching, gauging, and dissecting the words to extract their meaning. Simurgh also saw that the princess was not yet capable of this. 'Who would I be – to let you continue your way – with empty hands. Take – this gift.'

A feather landed softly on the princess' palm. In the light it shone with the colors of copper and green.

'One day – when fate has decided – that you are ready – for the answers to your questions – burn this feather – and I will appear to – fulfill your wish.'

Runak held the feather against the light. 'How do I know when that day has come?'

'What fate – has decided – falls outside – your knowledge. If your guess is wrong – your chance at the – answer will be lost forever – because once called – I am obligated – to answer.'

Simurgh's words echoed in Runak's head as she wondered what the creature knew about her but didn't make known. In the corner of her eyes, she saw the black and red of the snake and an intense sorrow for the lifeless body befell her. 'Allow me to pose one more question, wise Simurgh,' she asked.

Simurgh was placing her young on her back and getting ready to fly. She looked back and recognized the question painted on the princess' face. 'The creatures of – the darkness – will always – try to destroy – the creatures of the light – because the darkness can only exist – where it swallows the light.'

'And what are we?'

Simurgh spread her large wings and covered the field with her shadow. 'The world of humans – and animals – is nothing but – the shadow of that eternal battle. Find the darkness within yourself – and you will find the light – princess of the young kingdom near the Zagros.' She flapped her wings, almost blowing the two humans away, and took flight.

Runak remained with only the feather in her hands and an echo of words. The encounter had unleashed questions in her she didn't even know existed. The world had been revealed just enough to realize how much remained concealed. Akam had not been able to utter a single word during the conversation, both due to respect and awe. The princess was as holy to him as the magical creature that spoke to them. Listening to their exchange of thoughts, he felt in the presence of exalted beings.

They continued their journey, left the open field, and made their way through the vegetation. The distance to their thoughts narrowed and little by little they fell back into the stream of their consciousness until they were completely themselves again. Their surroundings regained their original character, instead of the possible experience it had become in their trance. The events with the magical Simurgh distorted until both wondered what they really had experienced and whether the amalgamation of shapes hadn't been an illusion of their thoughts. Did the events truly happen as they remembered?

The princess felt around in her pocket and discovered the feather, a tangible assurance that she could anchor to those fantastical events that seemed to race out of her memory.

6

The stillness of the forest slowly made way for the clamor of civilization. The sounds of hooves and hoarse men's voices reached them before they saw the men themselves. The road next to the forest was frequently used by merchants and farmers that sold their wares and families doing their shopping. Badinan was built on a high plateau. The city walls could be seen from the surrounding grasslands from afar. Its imposing gates even more so.

They passed the gathered mosaic of merchandise and passerby's and at the bottom of the steep path to the city gates, they at last saw how imposing the walls were. And how well guarded.

Akam took in the environment and memorized each guard. 'Princess, you would do good to cover your face here. Undoubtedly there will be people here who might recognize you.'

'We will not let the will of others rule over us, Akam.'

The warrior understood her point, but his pragmatic attitude granted him no respite. He also knew discussion was pointless. The princess possessed a stubborn quality. When she had decided something, it was thrown out into the world like an anchor and obligated everyone in its path to conform to it.

Within the walls, the city was full of life. The people had begun the second part of their day. When they returned to their stalls after the afternoon rest, they worked on into the softer evening sun. The scent of roasted meats and the merchants' voices tirelessly announcing their wares filled the surroundings. At the stalls they sold fruits, sweets, prayer beads, clothes, and much more. The blend of shouting salesmen, roasting sunflower seeds, and hookah smoke created an overwhelming aura. The stark contrast with the stillness of their journey required some getting used to.

The two bought a pack of sunflower seeds and pistachios and walked through the bustling city looking for the right teahouse. They ran into a crowd that was listening intently to an old man on a pedestal. He lay comfortably on a carpet, his head rested in one hand and in his other hand he held a hookah, which the locals called a nergele. His face was half visible because of the big white beard and turban on his head. The man took a big puff and exhaled enough smoke to momentarily fully obscure his face. 'Today I want to speak with you about courage.'

He paused until the light in the eyes of his audience indicated they had brought up their associations with the word courage from their memories. 'What is courage, younglings?' he asked and took another puff, awaiting their response.

The sounds from the crowd didn't grow beyond a buzz amongst each other before being swallowed up by the sounds of the bustling market.

The old man looked surprised. 'Where is your answer, younglings? Or have you not only lost the meaning of the word, but courage itself?'

The discussion amongst the crowd continued. Eventually a cautious voice rose up. 'Wise sir, each day you present debates with such questions, only to lure us with your sly tongue to the outcome you have already thought up from the onset.' With the eyes and attention fully vested in him, he grew more assured and louder. 'We appreciate your wisdom, but why don't you give us your wise lesson without having us walk in circles? Our wives and our plows await us, and our tardiness pleases neither them nor the harvest. So, tell us your answer so that we, filled with this new wisdom, can immediately apply this courage.'

The crowd buzzed with agreement. The request was mirrored in the reactions of the crowd and repeated until they demanded an answer in unison.

The bearded man broke out in a roar of laughter. 'And will you also be satisfied if tonight I lie with your beloved?'

Confusion spread among the crowd.

'And if I speak to you of the softness of her skin, the sweetness of her kiss, and the loving words she sent my way? Will you be as fulfilled with my answer as if you yourself had spent the night with her? Or would you call me a thief and despise me for robbing you of the blissful revelation of her body by telling you about such a magical night?'

The crowd looked at each other perplexed and they could only respond by sweeping the first proposal off the table.

'Come now, younglings, what you would not leave to another in love, do not leave to another in matters of the mind. Let us, as lovers, engage in the plays of the mind until she yields her gifts.'

He took another puff of the nergele and waited patiently until he was sure that all eyes were aimed at him. 'So, I ask you once again: what is courage?'

Moved by the plea, one of the attendees reacted. 'Brave is the one who isn't afraid, who perseveres and doesn't let anything stop him, one who looks death in the eyes and laughs.'

The group nodded in agreement.

Their teacher also nodded, while blowing out new smoke. 'Such a person can indeed be called brave. But isn't the one who perseveres in their quest despite their fear even braver? The one with fear has an extra obstacle to overcome: himself.'

The people once again turned to each other as they discussed whether the sage's words made any sense. The man himself looked at the crowd and saw an armed man next to a horse on which sat a young girl. 'Warrior with the mighty stallion! It seems my words are not convincing. You obviously have more at your disposal than just words. Tell us whether the brave look at death without fear.'

Akam was surprised that he had been picked out so easily and at the same time became worried. He had been keeping a close eye on the number of guards in his line of sight so far – and they on them as well. But the sage's questioning invited him to turn his experiences into words. 'Those who do not fear death do not hesitate to run into her bosom. I don't know if that makes them less brave, but it is only the living who can be brave.'

Akam's answer brought a more direct character to the wordy exercise, for which the old man thanked him.

'Maybe it is wise perseverance? Brave is the one that perseveres wisely.' Another said in an attempt to bridge the two statements.

'An excellent addition,' the sage retorted. 'But we are not looking for courage just on the battlefield but in all facets of life. Is a rich man brave when he wisely perseveres in spending his fortune?'

The man continued his argument while Akam disentangled himself from the captivating character of the questions. To his shock, the guards had, in that fleeting moment of carelessness, cleverly repositioned themselves and blocked their escape routes. Seven soldiers now stood in the passages between the crowds and another two behind them. A clean-shaven man, armed as well, walked towards them. The commander moved with a leisurely gait and without tenseness. Escaping without a fight was no longer possible, Akam estimated.

'We are honored and blessed with such a surprise, Your Majesty. To welcome you to our humble city, the princess and the king's champion, is a pleasure we are not worthy of. Agha Simko would love to receive you in his humble abode if that would please you.'

Under this veil of hospitality lay a menacing threat. The situation was precarious and having been discovered so quickly could only mean they were expected. Akam cursed himself for losing his focus with word games.

Before he could decide how to react, the princess said, 'Thank you, my good man. It is us who are honored to be received so hospitably in Agha Simko's domain.'

Akam followed her example. You give us great pleasure.' The decision had been made for him.

The escort guided them to a calmer part of the city. The houses had iron front doors, each with their own distinct pattern and color. Potted plants in various colors perched upon the entrances. The walls, on the other hand, gave away their singular architect by their uniform pale white color and height.

Arriving at the agha's large estate, Akam was asked to hand in his weapons. 'Merely a formality, I can assure you, sir,' the commander said.

The warrior hesitated and looked to his mistress for advice.

'The wishes of the host are to be respected. And with guards like this around us, we should be able to take a moment of rest, Akam.'

The warrior reluctantly undid his shield, sword, and spear. With the unraveling of each attribute, he felt his determination fade away. He thought relinquishing his weapons made him feel weaker, but in truth it was the repression of his true wish that sucked the life force out of him. As soon as he let go of his last weapon, he felt a blow to the back of his head. The world went dark.

The princess saw her safety fall into a thousand pieces. Upon Akam's fall her heart and body panicked. She realized her former invulnerability was due to the safety Akam offered her. She had naively believed that security was a facet of the world, instead of a fragile consequence of her being together with Akam. She burst into tears and cried, 'Let him go!'

The princess' voice had a forceful and determined character that made doubting her command feel like a breach of conscience. The men felt called to leave their target alone. They took their hands from Akam and awaited what was expected of them.

With a red face, Runak commanded the men. 'Go away and leave us alone!'

'Stand still, men!' a familiar voice called from the garden.

The princess looked up and saw her eldest brother. From the house he walked toward them with a few guards.

'Do not forsake your duty. You must protect the princess, not obey her,' he calmly said. With that, he brought the men back to their original duty. 'Take this traitor and leave us.'

The princess was shocked that her brother had already found her and realized she had smothered her own adventure. 'Why are you here, Rezan?' she asked, distraught.

He wrapped his arm around her. 'Runak, my sweet little sister. We were so worried about you. From one disaster you fell into another. Thank God you are safe. I hope that bastard hasn't done anything to you.

She pushed his arm away. 'I am as safe as can be, Rezan. Akam protected me. He doesn't deserve this!'

Rezan's joy changed into frustration. 'What are we supposed to do then? Run the risk of him going insane? He's a crazy man who abandoned his own wife and child and kidnapped a princess. God knows what else he is capable of!'

'He didn't kidnap me! I ordered him to take me with him!'

Rezan studied his younger sister's face to understand why she was defending Akam. He saw true sadness and a clear mind. 'Still, he should not have done what he did,' he said in a bid to end the discussion. 'Tomorrow we will travel back home. Everyone will be delighted to see you again. The king and queen are worried sick.'

'I'm not planning to go home, Rezan. Let Akam go free!' Runak commanded.

Her voice was full of vitriol, but Rezan could hear the despair that the guards could not decipher. He was not as easy to coax. 'Sister, that's no way to talk to your older brother.' He laughed affectionately. 'You're obviously tired and your kidnapper has confused you. Take some rest tonight, and you will feel much better tomorrow. And I promise we will take good care of him.' His voice was soft, but he was unrelenting. He put his arm around her shoulder and guided her towards the house.

Runak knew that she could not convince her older brother and allowed herself to be whisked away, knowing that Akam, seen as her kidnapper, would be punished for any further disobedience on her part.

7

The princess was settled in a private room to rest and prepare for the evening. Despite the comfortable and luxurious room, she felt like a prisoner, gazing through the bars of acceptable behavior. She realized that she hadn't run away from a place but from an expectation: an expectation of how she was to behave, who she was to be, and what she was to desire.

Runak had always been fairly free with how to spend her days, but the expectations were always present: in how her parents spoke to her, how her teachers tutored her, and how people looked at her. As if they were on the prowl, waiting for the right moment, like a predator in the shadows. Upon the announcement that she would inherit the throne, the predator now leapt from the shadows, bared its teeth, and Runak felt its breath, ready to devour her. That was what she was trying to escape.

Naively she thought by leaving the palace she would be freed from those expectations. It had worked for a short while, more due to luck than through wit. Freedom proved easy to gain but hard to retain. Defeated and burnt out, she collapsed on the bed and fell asleep.

That night she and her brother were guests at the agha's banquet. A festive atmosphere reigned and there was food in abundance. The princess played the role of a dutiful guest with equal measures of grace and composure. She replied politely to questions and maintained lively conversations. Nobody asked what brought her there, a question that was deliberately avoided to not embarrass her brother.

During the evening, the agha became more and more charmed by the young girl that conversed with viziers and men and women of nobility with the elegance of a queen. He couldn't help but desire her. The princess had caught his glance multiple times. It was the type of look she had seen glimpses of previously, arousing her curiosity. But they were so fleeting she could never make out what they meant. This time it was different.

The agha was big and his belly was well-filled. His voice was as coarse as the beard covering his face. Even when he wasn't talking, he made his mark on the space with his heavy breathing and musky scent. A bent dagger, decorated with gems, stuck out of the band around his harem pants and moved up and down with his belly whenever he laughed. For the first time he addressed his guests collectively. 'Friends, you honor me with your presence. But today we have an even more honorable guest than you respectable people.'

His wide look, with which he filled the room, then focused on Runak. 'Princess Runak, I've understood that you are the first in line to succeed the throne. An unusual decision and not one to be understood by a simple man like myself. More so, knowing that the heroic and competent Rezan, who also honors us with his presence, is your eldest brother. But King Sherwan is a wise man, wiser than all in this room and that is why I have become curious of your competence, so that we may get a glimpse of what your father sees.'

Runak saw all heads turn to her and stepped, despite her uneasy feeling, into her role. 'Of course, great agha. I hope to fulfill your expectations and those of your honored guests.'

'Excellent!' Simko clapped in his hands. 'Let's go to the courtroom. A peculiar affair awaits us, and we are all very curious about what the princess makes of it.'

At court, the princess sat next to the agha. Up close his scent was even more intoxicating and his eyes seemed to want to invade her. Runak felt discomfort in every fiber of her body.

Four men entered the hall. The oldest one stepped forward. 'Agha Simko, I request your judgment to judge these three thieves and have them compensate me for the damage they have brought upon me.' The men pointed at the other three. He was older than the three and dressed modestly.

'We're no thieves!' one of them called out.

'We are the ones who have been robbed!' the other shouted.

'We are three righteous brothers and haven't even seen his donkey!' the third shouted.

The old man turned around. 'How did you immediately know then that my donkey was blind in one eye, missing a tooth, and even what its load was!?'

The three brothers faced him with clenched fists. 'How dare you accuse us like that!'

'Calm down, calm down,' said Simko. 'Young men, why don't you tell us how you knew all those things about this donkey without having seen it?'

'Well, Agha Simko, we came across this man on the way back. But on our way, I had seen that the grass had been bitten on just one side of the path,' the eldest said.

'And I saw that some blades remained at each spot where there had been a bite, so that's why I knew it was missing a tooth,' said the middle one.

'And I saw that at a certain point the donkey had laid down, the right side was full of flies, and the left side was full of ants. That's how I knew what the donkey's load was: date syrup and grain.'

Agha Simko laughed and looked at the princess. 'What do you think, princess Runak?'

The princess had listened with fascination and had forgotten Simko's intoxicating scent for a bit. The relief was short-lived. 'It seems plausible, but they said they saw it on their way there. Where were they going?' Her answer was aimed more toward Simko than to the men.

'An excellent question,' he said and looked at the men. 'Where were you heading?'

The three brothers looked at each other, and with a nod, decided to tell the truth.

'Our father died years ago and left three bags of money, only to be used if our own money was gone.'

'This year, all three of us were to marry and to finance that, we went to the spot where everything was buried.'

'But when we got to the spot, we found just two bags!'

The princess felt Simko's gaze burn and felt forced to answer. 'So, you have been robbed. Do you have any suspects in mind?

'Yes, princess.'

'We do have a suspect in mind.'

'It's one of us!'

Simko once again took the word. 'Before we continue. You've also visited a judge to settle your quarrel. What became of that?'

'Oh, the judge fed us dog meat.'

'And his bread was foul.'

'There was something else that I would rather not repeat in the present distinguished company.'

Simko gestured for the judge to come forward. An old man with blood-shot eyes walked into the hall.

'Is it true you fed these three brothers dog meat and foul bread, good judge?'

The old man couldn't look up and remained hunched over. 'Yes, my lord, but not deliberately. They came to me with the issue of the donkey around lunch, so I invited them in. As soon as the table was set, they exclaimed that it was dog meat and the bread was foul. It was like they couldn't control themselves and were impulsive soothsayers.'

'What was the other thing they said?' Agha Simko said.

The old man hesitated, but Simko urged him to continue. 'That I am not my father's son, that I am a bastard.' The judge started sobbing.

'And? Were they correct in this judgement?'

'Yes,' the man said in between sobs. 'My baker admitted the grain was grown on an old cemetery, the cook admitted using dog meat and my mother...' He buried his face in his hands and started crying louder.

'Tell us what your mother said,' Simko said, visibly annoyed now.

'My mother said that my father couldn't have children and that I'm the son of a traveling derwisj who was our guest one night.'

Simko turned to Runak again. She felt his eyes crawl over her skin. The voices in the hall became dull, suppressed by the smoldering presence of his gaze. It befuddled her pores, like black smoke looking for an opening to invade.

'And, princess, what do yo...'

Runak jumped up. She couldn't handle the pressure anymore. 'I'm sorry. I'm sick.' She left without waiting for an answer, running to her room. Only then, when the doors closed, did she find rest. There she could shake off that nauseating feeling and the discomfort in her stomach died down.

'Excuse the princess, Agha Simko,' Rezan said after she left. 'She's had a tough journey. Allow me to judge in her stead.'

Not much was left of Simko's curiosity. 'Of course, dear Rezan. You are, after all, of the same flesh and blood,' he said in a bored tone.

The prince took space between the brothers and Simko. He stood in the center of attention and addressed the hall. 'If these brothers truly are impulsive soothsayers, then we will know who the thief is after this story.'

The people were immediately captivated and listened intently.

'Dear brothers, once there was a village where a boy and a girl were in love with each other. When the boy was old enough, he asked for her hand, but the family did not approve of him. Time and time again they refused his proposal. So, he tried a different route. He asked the girl to elope with him, but she refused because it would bring shame to her family. "But" she also said, "if I ever am to be married off, I promise to sneak out on my wedding night and run off with you."

After a while, her family found a suitable partner and she married him. But she never forgot her promise and sneaked out at night to the spring where her beloved would meet her. On the way there she was harassed by a thief who wanted her jewels so he could feed his family. The girl explained the situation and promised to return after she'd seen her beloved and the thief let her pass.

Her beloved waited for her at the spring, but when she arrived, he confessed that she was like a sister to him now. She's married after all, and it would be dishonorable to run away with her now. The girl walked back but first passed the thief to fulfill that promise as well. "By God! Why would he be more man than me?" he said when she explained what happened. "Even if my family doesn't eat for another week, keep your gold. Go home!"

Rezan stopped talking, knowing that all would want to know what her husband had to say.

'What an honorable man was her old beloved,' the oldest brother said.

'What an honorable man the thief turned out to be,' the middle brother said.

'What an idiot. If I were that thief, I'd swipe her gold and her lying self away,' said the youngest brother.

Rezan looked over to Agha Simko with a grin. 'There we have our thief, agha. The man who could not wait for another to make a mistake so he could toss away his mask of morality and still feel superior.'

II
Hope

8

The next day the princess, her brother, and their escort left for home, the place she had escaped weeks prior. Drowned in thoughts, the princess' mood became increasingly heavier. The carriage she was travelling in at least afforded her the comfort of shutting out reality.

Her brother tried to cheer her up but could not get a response. Rezan remained cheerful on the surface, but under his brotherly enthusiasm his cognitive dissonance was growing, which soon turned into resentment; why do you always have to be so ungrateful? A thought he did not articulate, as he talked about how delighted their parents would be with her return.

The princess noticed the shift in his voice, the forced tone, the stretch in pauses between his attempts to shift her mood. Above all, she saw the way he looked at her. A look that did not see her for what she was but for what she was supposed to be. A look that veiled her true self under the burden of expectations and tirelessly aimed to press her into that mold.

'Did I ever tell you of the poor shepherd who tried to better his fate?' he asked in a new attempt to break her silence. Rezan loved stories, and the crowd loved to hear them as much as he did to tell them.

'No,' his sister answered flatly and kept her gaze aimed outside.

Rezan leaned forward. 'So, there was once a poor shepherd. Each day he toiled in the sweltering sun, but despite his hard work, he remained poor. One day he met a man on horseback. The man was dressed in jewels and expensive fabrics. The shepherd looked at this rich person with envy and asked how he had gained such wealth. "Each day I work from sunrise to sunset, but I'm still poor. What is your secret?" he asked.'

Rezan wiped his forehead as if he were wiping the shepherd's sweat and then immediately changed character. 'The man on the horse was confident, and with a raised finger, answered, "It's very simple. Your peri, the fairy responsible for your fortune, is probably asleep. You must travel to the land of peris and wake her. Then all the riches will come to you with ease."

The shepherd immediately packed his bags and set off to the land of peris. He traveled deep into the mountains, where he was attacked by a bear. The shepherd convinced the bear to let him be, because he was on his way to the land of peris on important matters. The bear allowed him safe passage on the condition that he would bring a message to the shepherd's peri. "Whatever I do, I'm always gripped by an incessant stomachache. Can you ask what I should do to fix that?" Do you hear that, Runak? The bear had a request.'

His sister was still staring out the window without moving. 'Yes, I heard. The bear wanted to get rid of his stomachache.'

'"Of course I can!"' Rezan continued with enthusiasm. 'Said the shepherd and he went on his way. He went beyond the mountains and met a farmer who was just as intrigued by his destination. The farmer asked, "Can you ask your peri why nothing grows on my land? If yes, you're welcome to rest in my home tonight and fill up on supplies for your journey."

The shepherd agreed and the next day he left all stocked up. He traveled so far, he even reached a new kingdom. When the sultan of this great city learned of this unknown traveler, the stranger was immediately summoned to explain himself. This sultan too had a request for the shepherd. "Ask your peri why I never win in war. My army is large and strong, and my country is rich, yet I lose every battle. If you can ask this question, my finest horsemen will guide you to the sea."

The shepherd agreed and they immediately set off. Finally, they reached a large sea. The land of the peris was just on the other side, but the shepherd had no means to get there. Suddenly a massive fish appeared out of the water and asked the shepherd why he was sulking.

"On the other side of this water is my peri. I need to wake her up so she can get to work for me, or I will remain poor forever. But I don't have a boat to make the crossing, and I can't swim."

The fish had the perfect solution because he could easily get him to the other side. "But only if you ask your peri what I can do to stop this headache. It won't stop, no matter what I try."

The shepherd climbed on the fish and was brought to the other side. Here he found the peris flying around and very busy granting people riches and making their wishes come true. The shepherd looked around for a while and eventually found his peri sleeping somewhere in a bush. "By God, that's really her!" he exclaimed.

He woke her up and reprimanded her for her laziness. "You're absolutely right," the peri said apologetically. "I will immediately get to work for you."

The shepherd remained with his peri and passed on the questions that were entrusted to him.

"Your riches will certainly be awaiting you upon your return," she eventually said and sent him on his way.

The shepherd left with high hopes toward the shore. Finally, I will be able to enjoy a life of riches, he thought. He came by the fish, who greeted him with enthusiasm and asked him how it went.

"Amazingly! My peri is hard at work and my riches await me."

"And did you inquire about my headache?"

"But of course. Your headache is caused by two large jewels stuck in your gills. If you take them out, you'll be relieved of your headache."

The fish took out two shining diamonds from his gills and his headache immediately stopped.

"Do you want to take these diamonds?" the fish offered when they said goodbye. "They don't serve me anyhow."

"No, thank you," the shepherd responded. "My riches await me. I must hurry home!"

The sultan welcomed him and asked whether he had held up his end of the bargain.

"But of course and my peri knew exactly why you keep on losing. You pretend to be a man while you really are a woman. If you take up a lover, you will win all your battles."

The sultan undid all of her male garb, revealing a woman of dazzling beauty and said, "Take your place next to me as my husband and together we will conquer the world."

"No, thank you," the shepherd said. "Soon all my riches will come to me, so I really need to be going."'

Rezan paused his exuberant retelling and took a gulp of water. He hoped for a response, but Runak kept on stoically looking outside. She should by now have gotten the lesson. He decided to keep going. She'd understand when the story ended.

He put away his jug and continued. 'Eventually he reached the farmer. He too was curious about his stories and whether there was a cure for his stale land.

"The answer is simple," the shepherd said. "On the piece of land where nothing grows a treasure chest is buried. If you dig this up, the land will be able to grow crops again."

The farmer immediately got to work and found a chest filled with gold and jewels. He was so grateful he offered the shepherd half of his find and fertile land.

"No, no, thank you. My peri is hard at work and my riches await me. I must get going, or I might miss them."

When almost home, he ran into the bear and spent some time with him. "What incredible adventures you have been on," the bear said. "But tell me, did you ask your peri what I can do to fix my headache?"

The shepherd looked downtrodden. "Yes, I did, but I can't imagine it being possible, unfortunately."'

Runak sighed, knowing the end was near. 'I'm not like the rest of you, Rezan,' she said, her eyes still on the road. 'I didn't ask to inherit the throne, to be married, or to be stared at by everyone, like they're dealing with a fragile porcelain heirloom.

Her brother's face showed pity. 'Sister, we don't choose our fate, but we do bear responsibility for it. The only thing we can do is be grateful for the life we have, especially our lives. The people need us. Without us they are lost. Father, wise as he is, chose you to lead them. A bigger honor does not exist.'

The princess smiled meekly. He couldn't resist using that word. Grateful. 'Rezan, did you care to ask me why I left?'

'Because that insane man threatened you and left you no choice! Even now he's pitting you against your own family.'

Runak turned her head and looked at her brother for the first time. 'I was the one who convinced and manipulated him!' she snapped at him, as if to correct an injustice.

'Do not say such things, sis.'

'You don't care about me, just about your ideals.'

Now they both looked outside, as if their heads, like magnets, were being repelled from each other.

Eventually Rezan made another attempt to break the silence. With his gaze still aimed outside, he said, 'The bear began to lose hope…'

'Will you stop it with that shit story!' The magnets were polarized again, and they couldn't look away from each other. 'I'm not that little girl anymore who gawks at every story. You can't rope me in with your childish stories anymore!'

Rezan leaned back, defeated. 'No, you're not that little girl anymore indeed. You've been chosen as heir to the throne, an honor passing by your older brothers.' Sadness echoed in his voice.

Runak was upset by her brother's sudden emotionality. How dare he use a demand imposed on her against her? 'I don't want this either, Rezan. This was your role; you've worked towards this. Why are you accepting this so easily?'

'My job isn't to decide who deserves which role, sister. My job is to respect our father's decisions and serve our family to the best of my abilities.'

The magnets lost their poles. Brother and sister sat empty across from each other.

'"What you need to do," the shepherd said…' Rezan made another attempt.

Runak granted his brother at least the satisfaction of wrapping up his story and looked at him awkwardly. 'What did the shepherd say?'

'"Well, you need to find the biggest idiot in the whole world and eat him, but I have no idea how you're going to manage that." The bear rubbed his hands together. "Excellent," he said, and tore apart the shepherd on the spot and gobbled him up.' Rezan held up his hands like claws and swiped in the air.

Brother and sister shared a short bout of laughter.

Arriving at the palace, the princess was welcomed by a small group. The queen and some maids were present to bring them in. Her mother's heart could finally relax when she saw her daughter for the first time in weeks.

The princess was swung back into reality as soon as she stepped out of the carriage and saw her mother's teary eyes. A suffocating love that didn't allow her to be herself. A love that always aimed to keep her nearby.

Tears clouded Gelawezj's sight while she embraced her only daughter. She didn't see the resentment in Runak's eyes. 'My sweetest daughter. Light of my heart. You have returned to us, safe and well.' She wiped the tears from her eyes.

'I have never been unsafe,' the princess responded with her face aimed at the ground. How could she react with anger to such loving words? So, she limited herself to the tiniest thing she could say so that her true feelings would not cause her mother any further suffering.

The queen, surprised by her daughter's calm words, looked at her and didn't see any signs of sadness or relief. The dejected mood she misunderstood as shame. Who knows what that man had done to her? 'My sweet daughter, you don't have to worry. We love you, despite what may have happened or what may happen yet. You will never have to wonder whether you are welcome in the home of your parents.'

9

The following days melted together without Runak having any control over them. She fell into a dreamlike state in which a haze of busybodies took care of her every need as family members visited. The only thing she consciously did was occasionally shove food down her constricted throat to somewhat ease the hunger pains. She spent whole days gazing out of her window, watching people peruse around the palace square, the events of a world far from hers, a play she was merely a bystander to. She found consolation in the distance, in being absent, and slowly she withered away like a storm running out of rain.

One day a woman in a black robe walked onto the square. Like a shadow, she fluttered past the fountain towards the palace, with a little girl in her arms. Guards stopped her and an altercation commenced. The woman waved her arms in anger while the men tried to calm her. Her headscarf rested loosely on her head and revealed her golden locks, a sign of the impulsiveness underpinning her quest.

Runak recognized the locks, which seemed to shine like a golden aura in the full sun, as Hanar's. The princess could only feel pity for the mother, who was of course here because she had heard the news regarding her husband. From her maids, Runak had learned that Akam was being accused of kidnapping the princess and he would pay for it with his life. Apathetic and without feeling, she had taken in the news. What else could she do?

There was no way Hanar could count on mercy in an embarrassing matter that affected the royal family's prestige.

Still, she forced herself inside and stillness returned to the square.

These silent moments of solitude were the hardest for the princess. The lack of events to occupy her mind led to involuntary attention to her nagging conscience. Under the surface it banged against her mind to free itself.

Soon Hanar was escorted out again by two guards, who gestured for her to leave.

What did she expect? Runak thought.

Hanar seemed to make no attempts to leave and looked around, seemingly searching. Her daughter clung to her mother's garb and buried her face in her bosom.

Just go home before they do something to you, the princess negotiated in thought; he's withering away somewhere in a cell you will never find.

Only when Hanar looked up and their eyes met did she understand that the woman with golden hair hadn't come for her husband. Hanar's gaze took hold of Runak's numb mind and brought it back to the light, where she could not run from her debt. That woman with the golden locks, with a sobbing child in her arms, dared to place an obligation on the princess and brought her to acknowledge her blame and to settle them.

Hanar mirrored what the princess was ashamed of and took from her shadow the freedom to hide from it. In that one determined look, the princess felt the depth of her debt and the power to settle it.

When Hanar saw her plea reflected in its receiver she turned around and left without any further struggle. The two guards gave each other a confused look as they watched the sudden departure of this unwieldy woman.

The princess, swept up by her newfound strength and the gravity of the situation, landed fully into her body and stormed out of her room. The guards, supposedly stationed there to protect her, prepared themselves to shuttle the princess back to her room. But before they could recite their studied lines, the princess commanded them with the confidence of a zealot to open the door. Her winged door had been replaced by a cold and massive steel one that could neither be locked nor opened from the inside. No battering ram could break it, but against the determination of the princess, it stood no chance.

The guards, overwhelmed by the fierceness of the command, opened the door and allowed her to pass.

The throne room was filled with people discussing myriad issues of daily life in the kingdom. The king sat upon his throne, above the advisors, farmers, merchants, and various palace workers who were there on official business.

'Father!'

The king looked up at his daughter and all that were present followed his example. Runak stood at the entrance with fists bawled and rage in her eyes. Her small demeanor seemed to cast a shadow belonging to a giant.

'I demand that Akam be freed now!'

The audience tensely watched their king, who so openly was being challenged by his own daughter.

Sherwan understood that his daughter gave an order that only a king could fulfill, but that her rage was aimed at him as her father. But in this company, he could only be a king. If he wanted to keep his authority and win his daughter for himself, he would have to speak to her privately.

'Respectable guests and friends, for today we are finished. Your king requests rest to reflect on what we have discussed. Take your leave in the gardens or tend to other matters. Tomorrow we will continue.'

In a move where he gained the upper hand over the situation without having to deny or acknowledge his daughter's challenge, he had avoided a possible conflict in the eyes of those present. People would gossip, but nobody would be able to present anything tangible.

The guests walked past the princess and out of the room, with each paying their respect to the heiress.

Once it was just them, the princess began her plea. 'Akam has done nothing but follow my commands, father! He was obeying me. I convinced him. He has done nothing but protect me!'

The king listened without interrupting her and remained unmoved on his throne. Only when she had no more words left did he stand up and walk slowly towards his daughter. 'I know, my daughter. Akam is an honorable man and would never hurt you or throw his honor away. He was, until you spoke to him, loyal to me like no other. Of all the people that could have hurt you, he was the last. And of all people that could have kept you safe, Akam was the best.'

Runak's determination turned into despair. 'Then why does he need to be punished?'

The father stood in front of his daughter, with one hand on the hilt of the dagger on his side and the other resting on her shoulder. He towered over her, but Runak did not feel threatened. His hand on her shoulder was rough but softly planted. 'My precious daughter, a king is responsible for watching over all his subjects. He is the one who makes tough decisions for the safety and stability of his people. Matters of the heart, like my affection and respect for the brave Akam, must never compromise that. Our people must know that their rulers are honorable and trustworthy. That is the foundation which makes all that we do possible.'

Runak was in tears. 'But why does Akam have to be punished? I am the one that took him!'

Sherwan patted his daughter with the same dearness as when she was still a baby. 'That is exactly why. The people would never trust you if they knew the truth. They would never give you the chance to blossom into the wonderful queen that they need.'

The father, dressed as king, tried from the bottom of his heart to show the necessity of his decision to his daughter, but his plea backfired. After all, Akam was the one who supported her urge for freedom and now he was to be sacrificed on the altar of a responsibility that was imposed on her. Runak pushed her father's arm away and walked off.

The king's hope took flight. Her turned back shook his decision and in an attempt to not lose her heart as a father he, as unexpectedly for him as for the princess, relented. 'I'll spare him.' The words escaped before he could think them over.

Runak stopped and looked at him in disbelief.

Hurriedly he added a condition. 'Come with me to our place of origin. Where our forefathers unknowingly had to survive. Come with me to Shaneder so I can reveal why you are needed.'

The princess noticed the changed tone in her father's voice, a vulnerable one that made him seem human. He became a man capable of fear and a man that did not have all the answers after all. She agreed to go with him on the condition that nothing would happen to Akam.

Shaneder. A cold place only spoken of in hushed voices. A place the princess had never seen and never desired to see. What would they have to see there?

Not much later father and daughter left, accompanied by some guards, on horseback to the mountains that towered over their home. The Zagros stretched more than a thousand square miles. It separated the kingdom from the rest of the world as if it stretched its arms to protect them from the elements and specters of the past. Armies from outside had never been able to penetrate the rough environment and, either quickly or after great losses, gave up the hope of submitting the kingdom. These mountains were like a friend who had housed their forefathers when they were just uprooted children and generations later they still watched over them. What did they see? Were they proud of the kingdom founded in their shadow? Or did they still see the same fearful children? Did they have the mountain's blessings or just its sympathy?

The princess saw her home shrink as they climbed up further into the mountains. She saw the city walls and the forest where Hanar awaited the return of her beloved. She saw the Zab bend before reaching the Gara forest and, in thought, followed the path she had taken with Akam. A strange feeling grew in her stomach. A cramp she couldn't put her finger on, but which made her uncomfortable.

The king enthusiastically rode ahead when they were nearly there. They reached a large cave opening against the backdrop of a setting sun. The cavity they were standing in front of seemed to want to drag her inside and churned her stomach. Nonetheless, she did not let out a peep.

'And here they stood,' the king said, full of pride. 'Our forefathers, with nothing but grit, courage, and the will to help their companions create a new home.'

The guards remained outside while the king entered with his daughter. His enthusiasm was in stark contrast to his daughter's growing unsettling feeling. Each step further into the cave felt heavier than the previous. The nasty cramp slowly turned into a pain that made her want to crumble, but she couldn't let her father catch wind of her anxiety. Due to their feeble truce, she didn't want to risk any discord which Akam would be the victim of.

'My grandfather once brought me here, Runak. I was older than you and was to marry your mother. Your great-grandfather awakened in me the realization of the immense responsibility our line has taken upon itself. He gave me an important task that day.'

Runak searched for something to hold herself up to, as her father pointed at cave paintings that were supposedly left there by their ancestors.

'Ever since our departure from Shaneder, we have been embroiled in a cycle of war and peace. The clans live peacefully together until some trifle causes dissension. From one day to another they arm themselves and brothers and sisters take each other's lives. Hate and war rule the lives of man. Fear becomes the new king until one wins, and upon the enemies' corpses, heralds a new period of stability and peace.'

Runak only caught fragments of what her father retold, but those fragments only made her pain worse, as if she herself were being stabbed in such a war.

Sherwan, fully engulfed in his story, didn't notice anything and continued as he glided his fingers over the paintings. 'I never knew why. I didn't understand. Not even when I saw my own father hurry onto the battlefield or when I was forced to fight to protect my family.' He paused his hand beside a drawing of a beast impaled by spears.

'Peace came as unexpectedly as bloodshed and left me in confusion and frustration because I didn't seem to have gained anything. I lived in fear and saw in everyone a potential enemy in the next battle.'

Runak followed her father deeper into the cave through a narrow passage. They crouched with barely any room to turn around.

'Runak, the darkness of this cave follows us still. The fear of our ancestors lives within us and at the slightest threat turns brother against brother in a battle that can find its solace only in the subjugation of the one by the other. I have lived with that fear, day in, day out.

The small passage suddenly expanded into a large cavity. The king walked in and Runak remained at the end of the passage to rest a bit. The cramp in her stomach took hold of her as they walked further into the darkness.

'Until I beheld you. It took a while before I understood what I saw, before I saw what your mother immediately knew.'

Runak leaned against the cave wall and felt the cold, sharp stone crumbling under her weight.

'In you shines the light that can chase the darkness away. You, my daughter, are the one that can end this cycle of fear!'

With the last words of her father's hopeful plea, she felt a weight pulling at her body. The king turned around, and his daughter was suddenly gone.

10

A chill flowed over her skin, slowly caressing her back to consciousness. An ongoing shuffling filled her ears. The strange sounds remained indeterminate until she realized what her senses were perceiving.

Snakes! She was covered in snakes! The scaly, cold bodies slithered all over her as if they were trying to bury her alive. She covered her mouth to hold back the screams. Her eyes were wide open, but she couldn't see anything.

After what seemed to be hours, a small strip of light reached her iris. The light revealed the snakes, who were so plentiful they coagulated into a single mass to escape through the opening from where the light came. None of them seemed interested in the warm-blooded creature beneath them.

Runak tried to push herself up, but her hand found only broken pieces of wood and a splinter jabbing into her finger. Her hand shot back from the pain, and she carefully looked for a safer spot. Now her hand found a leather object. She pushed herself up and instinctively took it with her. Once standing, she figured she was holding a book. Carefully, she lowered each foot as she walked, so as not to trample any snakes or, worse still, startle them.

She leaned against the cold wall in order to look through the crack. With her weight against the wall, it moved ever so slightly, but with the aid of the mass of snakes who kept piling up, the wall began to open. The snakes hurried into the lighted room, and one by one, disappeared into small cracks in the cave walls.

Runak squinted while getting used to the new light. First there was only an arid brown. Next, she noticed flaming torches that hung on the walls. Then she saw a figure occupying her field of vision. Runak saw scales on a creature that looked like an enormous snake sitting on a throne. Her eyes traced the body upward, and she saw that the upper half was a woman. The orange hues of the torches contrasted with her white upper body and danced upon the cold scales of her lower half.

The chilling beauty kept Runak closely in her sight with pupils like razor-sharp slits in her yellow irises. 'How long has it been since humans dared to walk here?' Her voice was soft and grating at the same time. Her tone appeared bored, as she spoke with a sigh.

The princess, still confused, clung to the book. Pain raced through her body. 'Where am I?' she asked, squinting.

'Do you not know you are in the domain of your sworn enemy?' Something new had been added to the boredom. Surprise.

'Enemy?'

The snake woman slithered off her throne toward the princess. Close up, the princess saw how large she truly was. Her muscular body towered even higher over her than her father.

'I, Shahmaran, ruler of all serpents, am the sworn enemy of mankind, but in contrast to your deceitful kind I am merciful and allow you the chance of explaining yourself before I decide what to do with you.'

The princess felt the cramp swelling up again in her stomach. She held the book tightly. With clenched jaws she tried to explain how she ended up in the cave. 'I don't know where I am. The only thing I remember is that I fell and ended up here.'

Shahmaran saw the wounds, her wry face, and the blood dripping from her legs. She pitied the child, who obviously hadn't purposefully trespassed into her domain. 'I believe you've ended up here by accident, child. Come, let's fix you up so you feel better.'

The princess was guided through Shahmaran's domain, which seemed to resemble more of a cave system than a queen's abode. The hewed brown corridors twisted back and forth, emblematic of a snake. The walls were dull, and the corridors melted together from monotony. In a final twist the hallway widened into a large cavity. In the middle stood a warm water spring. A fog rose up and returned to the spring as droplets, as if it were stretching out to take in the minerals of the cave and create more space for itself.

Shahmaran invited the princess to lie in the water and wash herself. 'The water will heal your wounds and alleviate the cramp. Come to this spring every day in the coming days to soothe your cramp.'

Runak carefully walked into the water. At first touch she felt a warm embrace from the bottom of her toes rise to her head. Further into the water, her cramp gave way and every pore on her skin opened. She sighed deeply and her body relaxed.

Shahmaran kept waiting until the princess lay comfortably in the water and was just about to turn around when Runak asked her, 'Why do you live here so hidden away?'

The serpent queen hesitated. This child spoke to her with a unique innocence that made her pain wish to be known. 'It wasn't always so deserted as now. Once this place was my palace, a paradise filled with beautiful tapestries on the walls, and in winter it was as warm as a bath.'

'Then how come it's now so...' Runak hesitated to finish her sentence, lest she insult her host.

'Dull? Cold? To escape the treacherous dealings of man, we've retreated and broken contact with the outside world. Slowly but surely the flowers died, the tapestries frayed, and the once colorful walls faded into the dull labyrinth you see now. Only this healing spring retains her former glory.'

'It must be lonely here,' the princess said with closed eyes. The spring warmed her body with a softness that ebbed all her troubles away. The outside world seemed like a faraway dream and slowly she faded asleep.

Runak woke up slowly due to the scent of smoked meat and the aroma of cooked rice. She lay in a soft bed in a small room with nothing else but a nightstand. Lying beside her folded clothes was the small book with a brown leather cover. Well rested and feeling clean, her body felt safe enough to experience hunger. And the delicious scent led her to quickly dress and rush through the halls to a dining room with an enormous table filled with food.

At the table's head sat Shahmaran. 'Take a seat, child. This is how humans like to eat, right? Cooked and from cups and bowls?'

Her mouth watered and the exuberant display of food made her jump forward, but before the princess took a bite, she remembered Shahmaran's declaration of war on humans. 'Why would you feed your enemies?' she asked cautiously.

'Even though we are the enemies of man, we are not the enemy of every human. It is the rot in their hearts we despise, and you are still too young to have stained your heart with such sins.'

The pain in her words was enough of a sign for Runak that her host was speaking the truth. She set upon the food like a wild animal, making combinations between sweet, savory, and sour that she wasn't used to, but that strangely enough appeased her appetite.

After the worst hunger pains subsided and her reason regained control, her curious character resurfaced again. 'Why are you and humans each other's enemies?' she asked, rubbing her now full belly.

The serpent queen saw the princess for the first time as she truly was. Resolute and curious. Her piercing eyes in the light of the flickering torches were an invitation that even the most closed-off hearts couldn't ignore. And Shahmaran discovered there was still a part in her that hadn't closed itself off from the world and longed to be heard.

'Once upon a time, before my garden knew any shortages, a man fell, not any less spontaneously than you, into our world. His friends had abandoned him, hoping to take his riches for themselves. Jamisav was a gentle man. He found here a place that opened him to the mysteries of the world. And we enjoyed his stories of the world of man. It was so fascinating that they solely turned toward the sun, standing upright. They had no regard for the ground below them, from whose lap all that was necessary to sustain life was born.

One day, his homesickness began to resurface, and he wanted to return to his own world. I asked him to reconsider and that he still had so much to learn from us, but it was to no avail. He missed his world, and I eventually relented, but I had one condition. He was never to speak of what he had experienced here or where people could find us. If they knew, they would certainly hunt us down.

'Why were you so certain of that?' Runak asked.

'That's how it is with creatures of the light. In their urge to bring the light where it does not belong, they swallow up the darkness wherever they go. Their incessant drive to illuminate would destroy our mysteries.'

Runak remembered Simurgh's similar views about the creatures of darkness.

'Jamisav gave his word, and I believed him. Years passed and I forgot what he looked like. Until one day a voice I knew called me. But this voice had an all too nervous tremor. Jamisav had brought an army. My greatest fear had come true. The only human I had ever dared to trust had returned to take everything for himself. The only thing I could do was close off the exit and prevent them from intruding. Overcome by sadness, I fell into a deep sleep and when I woke up, my gardens had withered, the walls had faded, and life had left my palace. Ever since I swore that snakes and man would be each other's enemies forever.'

Runak intently listened and realized what this story meant for her stay. 'I presume that my departure here would also not be appreciated?'

Shahmaran looked away. 'You should first rest and give your body time to process the changes it is going through.'

'What changes?'

'Soon the world will lose her innocence, and you will leave behind your child years. The time to leave will come soon after.'

'And you decide when that time will come?'

Later, the princess lay lost in thought on the bed. Her body was still weak and after dinner she noticed it required more rest. What had become of Akam? What would become of her? How lonely Shahmaran must have been here. Were her parents worried? The thoughts came one after another, but one thought remained at the forefront: she was a prisoner.

She turned over and saw in the candlelight once again the bound book. The edges were frayed, but the rest were still in good condition. The pages were yellowed and filled with handwriting that was refined, like that of a calligrapher. She leafed through it and caught some sentences here and there. Slowly but surely, she began reading more intently. When it dawned on her what she had in front of her, she flipped back to the beginning of the book and read through the entire night.

11

Dear sons and daughters of our brood, lights of our hearts, blood in our veins, how cruelly have you been ripped from our nests, how humiliated you have been and how mercilessly stolen from the warm bosom of your mothers and the safe haven of your fathers. God almighty, release us from this torture. God, grant them peace in the afterlife. Their only crime was to be born in the storm of a decrepit king. My heart bleeds every day for you and each breath crushes my chest.

I hope that this message reaches you on time so that you at least may understand why you had to endure this hell. So that you may know what the source of your misery is and why we have been torn from each other. So that, despite it all, we may dream of the day we are united under one clear sky, one splendid sun. A day where your mothers will hold you with the same innocence as the day you first lay on their bosoms. We live on under this dark cloud, clamping to this one hope, to this one ray of light in a life of darkness.

The one who set your doom in motion is the tyrant King Zahhak. This fiend was punished for his deeds in the most sinister way. One day a vagabond appeared at his court. He entertained the king with stories from the farthest reaches of the world, magical spells and promises of eternal life. The greedy king, who had conquered all but time itself, was intrigued by this possibility. The vagabond convinced him that Zahhak was powerful and learned enough to attain immortality if the king would allow him to only perform one deed: a kiss on each of his shoulders. Zahhak, drunk on his own laudations, truly believed this vagabond had traveled the world to grant him eternal life and allowed him to step forward. The vagabond kissed him on both shoulders and disappeared like snow before the sun.

Where Zahhak was kissed, smoke rose up, black as the night. The smoke slowly thickened, and two snakes appeared, both just as black and in their eyes an insatiable lust was reflected. Zahhak became overwhelmed with fear, and in the horrified eyes of those present, their gruesome king became almost human in his mortal terror.

The snakes slithered steadily upward, growing from his shoulders. The hissing penetrated his eardrum, where it transformed into a feverish craving for brains. The king ordered his guards to strike the snake and so it happened. The hunger was stilled and the hissing ceased.

Zahhak went to bed reassured, but before dawn broke, he awoke from a sinister feeling. The two snakes on his shoulders had grown back in the night and slithered over his face. Zahhak panicked. He could feel their craving for brains. He could feel the impatience for the coming meal. He had to fight to retain his sanity, to avoid merging with the primal gluttony that sought to consume him. Once again, the snakes were sliced off. This time, the first signs of recovery appeared during the morning.

The king gathered all his viziers to uncover what kind of devilish magic had condemned him to this hell and how to put an end to it. One of the more cunning viziers proposed a potential solution to his predicament. The king had explained that with the recurring presence of the snakes, his headaches worsened, and a craving to consume brains grew – specifically, fresh brains. The vizier suggested that they could satiate the snake simply, by feeding them such brains.

The question of what actually entailed fresh brains was easily answered by the vizier: the brains of a child, young enough to not have reached puberty, so that their brains would not be dried out from toiling under the sun or tainted by desires of the flesh. Yet, also not much younger than that to ensure the brain's not being too small to still the hunger.

Only a fool or a monster would cheer for a cure more dangerous than the disease. Unfortunately, Zahhak is even worse. He is a monster surrounded by cowards. The decree to sacrifice two children for king and country was issued with such speed and fervor that it nipped in the bud any resistance lingering in the minds of those present. They agreed that the children should come from different families to spread out the suffering. And it could not be an eldest son, so as not to jeopardize the continuation of the family name.

That very day, two children were torn from their parents and prepared to serve as sacrifices for Zahhak's demons. Their young minds were old enough to understand what awaited them and they left their parents with the deepest sorrow, knowing that the king's will is law. They were blessed and received in the palace with honor and their life was ended painlessly.

Their brains were carefully removed without damaging their faces, while Zahhak's impatience grew, along with his lust, pain, and anger. Even the king could not undo the honor due to a martyr.

Finally, when the king was hunched over on his throne from the pain with his hands in his hair and the two snakes were being kept at bay by armed guards, the children's brains were ready.

As the aroma of the meal entered the room, the two black miscreants' forked tongues reached toward the dish of brains. Their gluttony spilled over to the king, who gestured for the servant to come closer. The snakes sank their teeth into the flesh and the king finally felt relief. Soon they had devoured the brains and gradually shrunk until they disappeared completely. The king was beside himself from joy. His mind finally was once again his own and, in his euphoria, he rewarded the two families generously for their sacrifice. The inconsolable parents were sent off with their restitution, not able to protest due to the shock.

Once again, the king went to sleep in peace. But, before the sun even rose, he was shaken awake. His face contorted in fear; the snakes slithered over his face and wrapped around his neck. The craving for fresh brains was now indistinguishable from his own mind. Panicked, he ordered the guard to immediately snatch two random kids off the streets and bring them to him. He would not endure this torment for another minute. The children were mercilessly and brutally beheaded, after which the snakes feasted on their brains.

And so, a dark age began where no child or family was safe. The king became possessed by his new insatiable companions and was convinced he would live eternally as long as he delivered them the brains of two children every day. I cannot remember a day when we didn't live in fear, not a day without a mother chastising herself on the streets in tears for the loss of her child. Beautiful children who had just begun to discover the world, to discover themselves. Children whose light was beginning to shine were stolen from their safe environment to end as feed. At first, they tried to conceal it all, and children were abducted from their beds in the dead of night.

But eventually, they were taken from their parents in broad daylight, who could do nothing but watch as their children were being taken away, never to be heard from again.

But even in the worst blood bath a light of hope can shine, though it's a bitter glimmer. The two men in charge of preparing the brains, God save their souls, were overwhelmed with feelings of guilt. They couldn't live with themselves for all the innocent blood they were spilling.

On one of those many days when two helpless and frightened children were brought to the kitchen, they devised a scheme. They hid one of the children and used the brains of a sheep in their place. No one knew if the snakes would accept it, but they were willing to take the risk.

Later that morning the two men stood before the eager king with a tray. His appetite over the weeks had intertwined with that of the snakes, making his mouth water at the sight of the tray. He too now partook in the despicable daily meals. The servants approached the gluttonous monsters on the throne. To further mask the ruse, they had mixed the two brains together and mashed the mixture, supposedly to make it easier to digest. The men feared for their lives, but the king's fixation on his meal saved them.

They offered the dish to the snakes. Face to face with the soulless reptiles, they saw nothing but four bottomless pits of gluttony. The snakes struck, not with the same eagerness as before, but still finished satiated. The king shared in their contentment.

The servants were overjoyed that their scheme had succeeded. But due to the reduced enthusiasm of the snakes, they dared not switch out both children's brains. Thus, it came to be that every day one child was saved, and another child was sacrificed. Without justification or system, one was doomed while the other was taken away by strange men to the vast Zagros. There, even Zahhak's darkness could not devour those children.

Those children are you. You have been saved from the clutches of Zahhak by angels condemned to be hangmen. It was those two, Armayel and Garmayel, who enacted a silent rebellion, endangering their own lives.

Yet, my heart weeps for you. In what darkness do you live? What has come of you? Without parents, without warmth, without direction. You have been thrown into the world before you were ready, burdened with the responsibilities of adults. Have you carved a path for yourself? Or have you been swallowed by the world?

My children have fallen victim to that vicious Zahhak. All four of them, beautiful and pure souls, were ripped from our warm home on the same night. A mother who lovingly tucks her children into bed only to wake up to an empty house loses her sanity and humanity. She falls into a deep pit where no light shines, where she can only survive by turning to the heavens and unleashing her anger upon it so that she does not drown in her tears. I spent an eternity in that pit, crying, cursing fate and filled with hatred. When there were no more tears to shed, my anger had also flowed away. Only the sorrow remained, like a stone that splits a river's course.

In that hollow, a faint light crept in far enough to pull me back. There, I found what bound me to all other hearts in this world. Yes, even to the rotten heart belonging to Zahhak. Only someone who is in pain themselves can, without conscience, inflict such pain. Will he realize, at the end of his life, how much joy his death will bring us? Will that realization make him beg for forgiveness? Will he repent?

The pain in my heart became a bridge to other hearts. We found solace in each other's arms, and slowly, the consoling took on a new character: a determined character and a wish to never allow something like this to happen again. To never again allow parent and child to be separated from each other. It is pain that gives meaning to this life, that guides us to our destiny. With this letter I hope to extend the bridge to your astray hearts. Let this offering of a dying heart light your way back home; let it guide you to where your source sprouts. Return, strong and nourished, and bring the light with you. Only your light will be strong enough to banish this darkness.

12

Runak awoke from a nightmare that left her gasping for air. A sigh of relief swept through her body as the events she had just been part of faded away. The leather-bound book lay on her stomach as a reminder of what she had realized before slipping into a world of pain and sorrow. She had fallen asleep while reading and now understood that this work contained the secret of their origins. Her hostess, the queen of serpents, must know more about this, Runak thought.

The hall outside her room bore no signage. She could turn right or left, but unlike yesterday there was no aroma to lead her. She decided to choose right and, after some walking, came upon another junction, with the same nondescript walls. She made another quick decision and hurried through the hallways until she lost all sense of direction and was frantically scrambling around.

'Shahmaran, where are you!' she cried out in desperation.

The hallways remained empty and silent.

'Shahmaran!'

Was this Shahmaran's attempt to keep her here? Forsaken to aimlessly wander within an endless maze of hollow caverns?

'You yourself caused the rivalry between man and snake!' Runak shouted in a desperate attempt to provoke her. 'It's all clear to me now thanks to this book!' Exhausted, she sank to the ground.

A snake emerged from a crack in the wall and slithered down her shoulder, across her torso, and onto the ground. Runak could only watch, frozen in place. Only when the snake was leaving did she realize she should follow it. It led her through the cave system until they arrived at the hollowed-out chamber serving as a throne room. She entered the space from the rear and saw only the back of Shahmaran's throne.

'Explain yourself, child of man. Such accusations I do not take lightly,' Shahmaran said as soon as Runak appeared.

'It's all in this book – how snakes drove King Zahhak mad!' The princess continued recounting the story as she paced around the throne, but Shahmaran was not acquainted with the snakes from the book.

'My snakes prefer to glide their bellies along the ground to stay close to the earth,' she said. 'These snakes, who grow into the air and desire brains, are no part of my kingdom.'

Runak held the book up and pointed it accusingly at Shahmaran. 'Weren't you the ruler of all snakes? How am I supposed to believe that you know nothing about this?'

'Not all are what their form implies. Magic can reveal many things, but it can obfuscate reality just as well.'

'Then let me go home. I must tell my people about this. They need to know where we come from.'

'You need to rest for another day.' Shahmaran's voice was scrambling, heavy, as if each utterance required effort, as if her attention was directed elsewhere.

She hesitated a bit too long to sound convincing and Runak used this to reinforce her demand. 'This is no place for a human, Shahmaran. I am needed where I came from.'

Shahmaran sighed. 'Even now I cannot charge my heart to chain an innocent human in a world she does not belong to.'

'You have my word that no one will ever hear of this place,' the princess said, hoping to convince her.

'So, it is said,' Shahmaran decided.

From the cracks in the wall two snakes came forth, each holding a cup.

'The only way out of here is through the spring. This cup contains an extract of my blood and this one holds water from the source. These two ingredients combined grant the drinker the ability to survive underwater for a long time. This way, you can swim to the secret passage through the spring and return to your world.'

Runak took the first sip and drank the tepid water. The second drink was black and seemed to be bubbling. She hesitated and looked up at Shahmaran with doubt.

'There is no other way.'

Although it was unclear what she exactly meant, Runak knew that no other options would be offered to her, and she downed the drink in one go. The serpent blood was bitter and burned in her throat. As soon as it reached her stomach, she let out a burp while her body protested. Her knees weakened until her feet gave out and she collapsed onto the hard, cold floor.

From the ground, she looked up and saw the barren walls transformed into a colorful kaleidoscope of moving patterns and figures, as if the lost tapestries had come back to life. The white Shahmaran was now multicolored, like a rainbow, but a dark shadow had drawn over her eyes. And thus, the betrayal revealed itself in the physical world; Runak knew she had been poisoned. With the little control she still had over her limbs, she frantically searched for the only thing that could save her: Simurgh's feather.

Shahmaran's voice echoed in the distance: 'I'm sorry, little one. You could've stayed here as my guest, but I can't let you go. Don't fight it. It will all be over soon.'

She writhed in pain as the poison penetrated deeper into her body. Everything inside her contracted from the sullen substance that seemed to burn through her stomach lining to terrorize the rest of her organs.

'I'm sorry.' The words escaped Runak's mouth like captives.

Now that her final moments had arrived, she was overcome by regret for not heeding the pain of her people. She regretted not picking up the torch of the generations before her. She regretted dragging Akam into her escapism. She begged for forgiveness for ignoring the desperate cries of her father and mother. Tears of pain mixed with tears of regret, and on that cold ground, gravel and sand clung to her wet face.

When everything she could regret had been uttered and swallowed by the earth, the pain also disappeared. And with the pain vanishing, her self faded away. She was no longer in the throne room with Shahmaran. She was nowhere. She was not. There was no time, no place, only colors, and endless patterns.

Slowly, the patterns began to take the shape of memories. First, those of herself, like when she carelessly ran after her father through the palace. He walked hastily and was surrounded by many viziers. He seemed so far away to her in those moments, like an unreachable mountain peak, by itself. The viziers morphed into steel pipes, trapping her father in a cage as he was paraded through the palace.

She also saw the joy on her parents' faces when she was born. She felt their hope for a safe life for her as her own hope. She went even further back in history and came upon the memories of her ancestors. Proudly, they descended on the Zagros, into the vast world and determined to leave their past behind. She experienced all the stories that had once been endlessly recited to her through the very eyes of the people who had lived them.

She went further back in time until she was a child standing in the kitchen of Zahhak's palace, frightened and confused, begging for her parents. She felt what it was like to be dragged away, without explanation or justification, to an unknown place, far from all she knew. She noticed how the child built a wall around their heart. How that wall was passed on to their own child, like a shield meant to protect them. She felt how the wall grew with each generation, becoming more refined, until the feeling of an open heart had become a strange and distant idea. She saw the succession of inheritance, now moving forward in time. She saw how each new keeper of the shield shaped it in their own way, expanded it, and passed it on as if it were a family heirloom.

Until, eventually, she ended up with her own father. She saw how the heavy edifice exhausted him, how he had hauled it around all his life and how much he suffered from it. Her father was undone from his royal garments, undone from the shadow that imposed demands upon her, and changed into a man stretching out his hands and crying out for help. 'Help me free these walls from their hold over my heart. Help me escape this darkness. Help me.'

Then there was nothing but emptiness. Soon, the sense of herself emerged in a black void. From the darkness grew the interior of a palace, filled with tapestries and beautiful tiles in ornate patterns. The hard ground she lay on vanished; the coldness became warmth. She was lying in Shahmaran's lap while the serpent queen gently stroked her.

'You're safe here, darling.' Her voice was soft, her tone warm.

Runak was in a dreamlike state, not entirely herself yet. 'Why did you close yourself off?' She asked it like a question in passing, like friends inquiring about an event.

Shahmaran stopped stroking her. 'I never closed myself off. Never.'

Runak slowly opened her eyes and saw Shahmaran's loving gaze. Her eyes were not yellow but green. Her voice was not heavy but exuded a somber calmness.

'I walked to meet Jamisav. It wasn't his fault; I knew that much already. He was forced by a vicious ruler to reveal my location because he wanted to claim my mysteries for himself. So, I did what every queen would do: I protected my kingdom. The king would receive my powers and my life if he would allow me the pleasure of using my venom to take revenge on Jamisav. At least, that's what I made him believe. He would receive my healing blood if he would administer my venom into Jamisav. In reality, both of them drank the opposite. I paid for this scheme with my life.

'With your life? But you're still alive.'

Shahmaran laughed. Gently, she lifted Runak from her lap and laid her back in the same position as she had been in before. 'The World holds both darkness as well as light, truth and mystery, and you, my dear, are the bridge between the two.'

The walls lost their luster and the tapestries vanished. 'You illuminate what is hidden and bring the two worlds together. But you are still a child and your vision is narrow.' Shahmaran's shimmering form faded and only the flickering torches remained. 'Open your eyes and see through the illusion.' The warmth was drowned out by the cold ground. 'See what is veritable.'

Runak's eyes flew wide open, and her pupils dilated to take in each glimmer of light. The cold Shahmaran with yellow eyes sat once again on her throne, eyes turned away from the suffering child on the ground. Her guest had stopped writhing in pain, and it would not be long before it was all over. The walls were solid, dull, and bleak once more. Shahmaran lost her colorful appearance and was once again entirely white, save for a faint copper-colored glimmer that seemed to shine from beneath her scales.

The princess pulled herself up and stumbled toward the throne.

'Do not fight it, child. It will only worsen the pain. The venom will do its work soon enough.' Her voice was heavy again and filled with a ghastly detachment.

Runak kept stumbling forward.

'There is nothing you can do,' Shahmaran said when the princess stood in front of her. From her throne, she looked down on the fragile, small girl, barely still alive.

Runak stretched out her arm toward the copper glow that guided her like a beacon. Her hand passed through the scales and grasped Simurgh's feather.

Shahmaran's appearance crumbled into hundreds of small snakes, which slithered away in fear through the holes in the wall. However, one snake remained, along with the feather, in Runak's grasp. The illusion was broken.

'Not all are what their form implies,' Runak said. 'Shahmaran died long ago, and you stole her place.'

The snake had beige and pale-yellow scales in a pattern that would not stick out in a mountainous environment. They were rough, and near her eyes, they curved upwards as if being small horns. She struggled and tried to bite Runak, with eyes glowing red with fury. Her body coiled and twisted around the princess' arms, but she was powerless. Runak threw the snake against the wall and ignited Simurgh's feather in a torch.

The snake screeched in anticipation of what was about to happen and rushed toward the torch, but the princess kicked her back.

'Attack her! Kill her before she brings us to ruin!' the snake commanded, but none of the other serpents obeyed her order, recoiling in fear of what was to come.

'Not everyone with a crown is a queen,' Runak said.

As soon as the feather burned up and the fire died down, the corridors thundered, and a deafening explosion rang out. The princess crouched down to protect herself from the flying debris.

When she opened her eyes, the walls shimmered in Simurgh's colors. The sun shone through a newly formed gap in the wall and reflected off Simurgh's body.

13

Simurgh had struck like a bomb and filled the serpents' cavern with her majestically colored body. 'You have summoned me - princess - and I have answered.' Her voice reverberated throughout the cavernous space. 'It appears - I am saving you - from the same plague - you once saved me.'

The princess rose to her feet. 'I am ready for the truth of the world, Simurgh.'

The snakes frightfully peered from their burrows up at the mighty Simurgh. She met their fear with contempt.

'Only at - the moment of confrontation - does a human know - if they are ready,' Simurgh said, as she lowered her head for the princess to climb onto her back and spread her wings wide.

'Wait!' Runak exclaimed, as if forgetting something. 'You should all know that Shahmaran willingly gave up her life for Jamisav.'

'Do not lie, human!' screeched the false Shahmaran.

'She does not lie - Jamisav was forced,' Simurgh added.

Runak realized that Shahmaran had lost her life outside her palace. 'Simurgh, you know all that transpires in the light!' she said excitedly. 'You know why Jamisav betrayed Shahmaran.'

The other snakes curiously awaited what Simurgh would say from their burrows. She looked around and decided to answer the questioning eyes. 'You know that - anyone who spends - time here - begins to resemble a snake - and it is water - that reveals their scales.'

Runak looked at Simurgh with a questioning gaze. What could that mean for her?

'This was also known - by the vizier of Jamisav's king - and when that same king - befell an incurable disease - he sought Shahmaran - whose healing powers - could cure any affliction. All subjects - were forced - to come to the bath house. That is how Jamisav - was ultimately discovered. The king used - Jamisav - to lure Shahmaran outside - and there she found herself surrounded - by an army of men. Your queen manipulated - the king into mistaking her venom - for her blood - and the rest you already know.'

Simurgh glanced at the overturned cups. 'It seems - that her scheme - remained hidden - even from her subjects. You thought - to poison the princess - but instead you unwittingly granted her Shahmaran's powers.'

The princess turned to the frightened fake Shahmaran, reduced to her true, small form. She extended her hand. 'The world of man has done much harm to you, and you have done so to us. Is it not time to bury the hatchet?

The serpent seemed for a moment to consider agreeing and inched toward the edge of her burrow, but at the last moment changed her mind. 'Let's not deceive ourselves. If I join you to the world of man, I will not forget what they did to our queen, and they will not forget their loved ones bitten by us. There will always be pain wandering in our hearts and driving us to mistrust one another. So, let us accept the past for what it is. I do not need to see the light and you do not need any serpent friends.'

She retreated into the hole and disappeared along with the other snakes into the walls. An empty cavern remained. The torches were shattered and Shahmaran's throne lay reduced to rubble.

Runak raised her hand as if to say goodbye, in an empty cave. 'Godspeed, enemy of man.'

In this world something can never be what it is not. Anything that rejects its essence will see its world wither and its very existence vanish. The snake had never been able to accept losing Shahmaran, losing her queen. So, she created an illusion, first and foremost for herself, so she would not have to live with the truth. The illusion lulled her into slumber, for only asleep and numb can we deny the truth. In a dreamlike state she lived on until she even forgot who she truly was, until Shahmaran's palace withered into a lifeless grotto.

Simurgh could barely stretch her wings, yet she managed to soar through the newly formed opening with breathtaking speed. The princess clung tightly to her feathers as Simurgh flew high above the Zagros.

For the first time, she looked down on her world and saw how small it was. Everything she had ever known was visible in a single glance and paled in comparison to the vastness of the wider Zagros Mountains range. And beyond the Zagros, far beyond, a dark cloud loomed over a region that Runak could only designate as the place her ancestors had come from. In that moment she resolved to one day journey there and drive out the darkness that lingered.

'Princess – bury yourself in my feathers – and do not emerge – until I tell you.'

Runak dove into her thick feathers until she could not see or hear anything of the outside world. All she felt was the soft, downy texture of Simurgh's plume and the serenity of the silence. Suddenly, she was pushed back by a powerful force. This lasted for several minutes, after which she felt completely weightless.

'Now you may – emerge.'

The princess saw a vast emptiness and experienced a stillness that made her doubt her hearing. In that emptiness, a blue orb floated. Her eyes widened in amazement. 'What am I looking at?'

'That is the World – where you live princess. Everything that has ever transpired – and everything that – ever will transpire – all worries – and all that you look forward to – takes place there.'

From this distance, there was no Zagros left, no kingdom, and no dark cloud in the distance. There were no buildings, rivers, or humans. Only a blue orb, covered with white clouds, floating in black emptiness.

Simurgh stood out against the gray expanse like the last tree in autumn, yet to shake off its colorful leaves. 'And the truth – of this World – is simply that she lives – and grants us life. The sun – impregnates her soil – and from her warm embrace – grows all creatures – and all that they require – for life.'

The princess looked ahead from Simurgh's back. 'This... lives?' she asked in surprise. 'But how does this live? It's just stone, earth and water. People live, animals live, and yes, even plants live. How can the earth itself live?'

Simurgh turned to the princess, her large eyes taking her in. 'The truth – of the World – cannot be given – only lived,' she said, harking back to her earlier warning. As if hoping the princess could still grasp some understanding in her eyes, she looked back at the globe and continued, 'you worship humans – you worship gods – you fear them – love them – work for them – and wage war – against them. But in your drama – you forget – that life has – been gifted to you. And just as freely – as it has been gifted – it will be reclaimed – and every life will return – to the womb that bore it.'

The princess listened to Simurgh while trying to understand what she meant. She tried to take in the hovering orb completely, to experience it in its entirety, but she caught herself looking for a glimpse of her kingdom.

'The womb that bore us? The snake spoke of this as well. That humans forget that the soil bears all.' Runak was surprised that so-called beings of light and beings of dark would say the same about the world.

'All beings – trace their origin – back to that same – World. Light or dark – eventually all find – the same end – and the same source.'

The princess continued to watch in awe at the lifeless globe. Now, beneath the clouds, they could distinguish which parts were water and which land. A shadow passed over the globe. Night was coming.

'The World allows – humans to grow – and they forget – that everything has been given to them – every meal – every victor – even every stone. Time and time again – she reminds them – by reclaiming all her gifts – with fire and water and wind – she opens herself – and swallows everything – they thought they possessed – be it flesh or stone – wood or steel. Everything she takes – back inside her – and in her shadow – they begin anew – first in fear – but soon – hubris follows – until they once again – forget and – confuse their gifts – for victories. The drama – of your life – is but a fleeting dust cloud – on the soil of the World.'

The princess thought about her family and Akam. She thought about her father's heart and about her urge to leave her childhood home. She thought about the emptiness in her life, the void she only felt when learning about her history. A thought made its way to her vocal cords. 'But it is important to me.'

Simurgh turned her head back closely toward the princess. 'Important – to – you?'

'Yes, it's important to me,' Runak repeated, with more certainty now.

'What is – important – to you?'

'My family, my fears, my ancestors, and my people. The suffering they have endured. The beauty they hold inside.' And then, as if she wrapped it all into one word: our drama. It is important to me.' Her voice was resolute.

Simurgh flapped her wings, arranging her feathers. 'Princess of the young kingdom – by the Zagros – your drama – is your path. Allow me to do you – one last favor. Your father – is about to – execute – Akam the warrior – for the crime – of kidnapping a princess. Are you ready – to repay your – debt to him?'

Runak nodded. She knew what she had to do and no one would need to become a victim of it.

With the princess safe in her feathers, Simurgh pushed herself off the moon. Gravity gently released her, and they floated for a time in the space between heaven and earth. Both enjoyed the calm and peace before the World reclaimed their presence. The floating turned into a falling due to the pull of the earth. As if greeted with scorn, they were surrounded by a heat found only in the deepest parts of the earth's molten core. Simurgh's scales expanded and moved to her underside, where they provided protection against the searing temperature. The calm weightlessness was replaced by the intense trembling of Simurgh's body, which did everything it could to avoid imploding under the atmosphere's pressure.

As quickly as the trembling began, it was over. The World had accepted their return and granted them safe passage. Simurgh dove towards the kingdom.

14

In the human kingdom, the inhabitants had gathered to hear their king's verdict and lament the downfall of a hero. A warrior, who had earned the right to stand beside the king and protect him, had lost his way. He now stood in the palace courtyard to hear his final judgment.

Dried crusts of barely healed wounds lined Akam's cheekbones. His battered face was discolored and distorted. He struggled to keep his balance on the bucket with trembling legs as the rough rope chafing around his neck created fresh wounds. Even in his final moments, they allowed him no rest.

'For abdicating his duties, kidnapping the princess, abandoning his wife and child, committing his treason against King Sherwan, high treason against the people, for this, the court sentences Akam, the warrior, to hang by the neck until death,' the executioner declared to all those present, like a play that no one had rehearsed but whose script everyone knew.

The crowd screamed and roared vulgarities at the hero, who had fallen from grace. He had betrayed his honor and, with that, forfeited his humanity as well.

The king showed himself as merciful from his balcony above the crowd. 'Akam, you were like a son to me. I took you into the bosom of my kingdom. Tell us what you have done with the princess; let her not fall victim to your actions.'

'I don't know where she is,' a hoarse Akam replied in a desperate attempt to be believed. 'I haven't seen her since I was struck unconscious.'

The king, determined to showcase his authority so that no subject would dare believe his omniscience could be evaded, was not satisfied with his answer. 'If your king is not enough to compel you to tell the truth, then do it at least for your wife and child.'

Akam had endured the torture with an iron will. But the sudden sight of his wife and daughter, crying in sorrow, their faces filled with horror, broke him. Salty tears rolled down his face, clinging to the scabs and wounds, as if even his grief was not allowed to flow freely.

'Show them in your last moments that there is still a shred of honor within you, so that they at least can say that the most important person in their lives died as a man.'

Akam's will was broken. What was his sense of duty and honor good for if he couldn't even protect the most important people in his life? And with his broken will, the fire in his heart began to dim. But before the fire disappeared, it was fanned one last time by aan unexpected gust of wind.

Simurgh had turned their free fall into a glide with a flap of her wings. She calmly landed on the palace, overlooking the square where the execution was taking place. Each movement of her wings felt like a squall on the open sea, forcing the people to brace themselves to remain standing. The magical bird shimmered silver in the moonlight and blinded those present. On the back of this creature stood a human figure. Outlined against the full moon, only a silhouette was visible, with her hair freely flowing in the wind.

'Hear me, wise King Sherwan! Your daughter has returned to banish the darkness!'

The spectators' eyes had now adjusted to the darkness and the silhouette revealed itself as the missing princess. Both the members of the royal family and the assembled crowd watched in awe.

Only the queen noticed that her daughter was no longer a child. She had taken a significant step in her development. The world she lived in was no longer a matter of course or innocent. She was ready to fulfill her destiny. That's why the queen was the first to speak. 'Daughter of my heart, pride and glory of our kingdom. Finally, you have returned to us!'

Simurgh lowered her head so the princess could join her parents on the balcony and flew off. Runak embraced her parents, consciously for the first time in her life. Her father felt her arms around him and the devotion in her embrace. His daughter was finally ready to embrace her home.

'I'm sorry father and mother. I've forsaken you. By running away from you, I was running away from myself. By rejecting my birthright, I denied the pain of our ancestors. I buried your pain and hope because I wanted to be free. But I understand now that none of us are free until all of us are liberated from the shadow of our past.'

The princess filled her parents' hearts with the love of her words. For the first time in their lives, she gave them the feeling that they could trust her. Despite their conviction that she should be the future heir, they had compulsively tried to persuade her, guide her, steer her. That was no longer necessary.

As if the roles had reversed, the princess reassured her father. 'Today, you won't lose a warrior, father,' she said and turned to face her people. He tensed at the realization that he would not have the final say in what happened here, that his authority was being challenged. For the first time the king was confronted with the implications of succession.

'Relax, Sherwan. Entrust your burden to the light of our lives,' his wife said, sensing his tension.

And having faith in his wife and his daughter, the king allowed Runak to take her place as the future ruler of his kingdom.

Akam still stood on that platform, his neck inside the noose. His wife and child had joined him and looked up at the princess, who, in the recent past, had once stood before their home as a mere child.

'It is my turn to protect you,' she whispered to him. Through her naivety, she had put Akam in danger, and now she would make it right. But that moment had not yet come.

'As long as we can remember, a threat has lurked within our hearts.' The princess' words struck the audience like a lightning bolt from the sky. 'A shadow we cannot banish or comprehend. It's like a contagion, passed from parent to child. It has lived among us for so many generations that we no longer even notice it. It is the tapestry on our walls, the furniture in our houses, and the stalls at our markets. It slips past our consciousness, from where it can grow in the darkness and control us.

I know you catch a glimpse of it when the world is silent and no one is around you. That shadow abandoned our ancestors as children in the caves of Zagros, and that same shadow prevents us today from dreaming of a brighter future.'

The people listened as if they were being reminded of a forgotten event from their youth or of a distant dream. The princess spoke openly about something that was never addressed openly, something that was never acknowledged.

'But here, in this book, the origin of our people is written. I will tell you exactly who that shadow is so we can drag it out of the darkness and see it evaporate in the light. Far beyond the Zagros, there lives a cruel king. He takes the lives of his subjects without discrimination to feed his devilish nature. But angels were able to partly elude his dark magic and save one child each day.

Those pardoned children were our ancestors. They were torn from the safety of their families and by a miracle their lives were spared. They were saved from fate and gave rise to us. We have never been abandoned or cast aside. We are the saved hope of mercilessly oppressed people! We are the light in the shadow! Our pitiable state came from the wish of our fathers and mothers to have us live!'

The suppressed fears of the listeners rose to the surface. The real threat of being stolen away had lived on as an undetermined fear, like a shadow. Now that the light was shining upon it, people panicked. Above the murmurs, Runak's voice rang out like moonlight in a dark house. 'Listen carefully, my servants! Do not shun the fear but be hopeful for the light! Your princess has not returned from the heavens to strike fear into you. Heed my words!'

The crowd quieted down. All eyes were fixed once more on the balcony with the princess who spoke like a monarch. Runak waited until she could hear the wind singing again.

'It is clear to me now how far the wisdom of our king stretches. He never lost sight of the darkness. And he saw whose fate it was to bring the light here. That was my fate! I have returned from the heavens solely for that reason. I have seen the darkness with my own eyes, and our mission is clear. We will return to the devil of our past and banish the cruel king. To that end, I will ascend to the throne as your queen!'

The princess looked down at the exuberant faces of her people. Soon, she would succeed her father, who had placed an arm around her, and lead them to the origin of their existence. She would, face-to-face with the horrors of the past, set right what her ancestors had not been able to.

With the trust in her at its peak, it was time to settle her debts. 'Let Akam the warrior go free at once! His only crime was his courage to follow me and see what I had not yet seen.'

Akam's chains were removed, and he bowed to the princess. He embraced his family and was escorted off the square.

The people's origin story was spread to every corner of the kingdom after that day. The traveling singers, called dengbej, told of how the princess had journeyed to the deepest depths of the world to discover, in the darkness, the origin of their existence. They sang of how she had been brought back by an angel with the task of wiping the terrible King Zahhak from the face of the earth. The dengbej spared no superlatives in weaving his demonic nature into their tales.

One moment, he was as large as an elephant. Then, he was as ugly as the night or had three heads, three mouths, and six eyes. He could seize you in your dreams and preferred eating naughty kids. The shadow took on a definite form, a form that was to be destroyed.

The people welcomed the new history like a long-lost friend. And they were stirred by the idea of the devil being struck down by themselves. Even the more distant and hostile clans united under one banner against a common enemy. And their leader was the princess, who had reunited them with a past unbeknownst to them.

It was a time of great reconciliations, of forgiveness, of comrades turned into enemies finding each other once more.

Knowing that their ancestors had endured the same tragedy, their present rivalries crumbled. It was also a time of preparation and anticipation. All the clans worked toward the primordial battle, the fight in which they would take revenge for what had been done to them and, once and for all, free themselves from that slumbering fear, from that shadow nestled just beyond their consciousness.

III
Spring

15

Before the united clans of the kingdom could go into battle, the princess would need to become a queen – and a queen must have a king by her side. Herein, all the warrior lords, noblemen and those in important positions saw an opportunity to elevate their status. From across the kingdom, they traveled to the palace with their eligible sons to present them to the princess.

Runak had never been interested in men and even now she could not understand why the maids swooned over every man on horseback who showed up overly dressed in daggers that were so ornately bejeweled they'd become unusable.

'Oh, princess. You're so lucky to have your pick out of all these handsome and well-to-do men. Any one of them would die for you without a moment's notice!' a maid said, with deep sighs and flushed cheeks, as she brushed Runak's hair.

'But I don't want them to die for me. A dead king is of no use to me,' the princess protested, not understanding what the maids, who had experienced the charms of being courted, meant.

Now that she had passed the first phase of womanhood, it was time for her mother to educate her about her coming role as a wife. The princess reacted with disgust to everything that took place within a marriage. She wanted to marry for practical reasons, to have someone by her side and thus give legitimacy to her position. Consummating the marriage or bearing children had never even crossed her mind.

'If you find the right man, you will understand, my dear,' the queen lovingly said.

'Well, I don't think so. With their pungent scent and sweaty bodies, they're like animals. A marriage of convenience to fulfill my role – I think that would be best for everyone.'

The maid laughed. 'But princess, how truly delightful it is to be grabbed by those beasts!' She noticed the queen's disapproving gaze and stammered an excuse. 'It's important that you choose a man who will take good care of you. And someone who doesn't have too many demands. Men can be quite demanding.'

The queen gazed out over the square at the arriving guests. 'First, you choose a husband, and only second, a king. Choose someone with whom you can leave all politics aside.'

'Exactly! You need to choose someone who makes your heart race, a romantic, with flowers. And a handsome one!' the maid continued.

The princess doubted more and more with every description about her decision to marry quickly. 'How did you and dad meet?' she asked her mother to change the subject.

'At our wedding.'

The two young ladies were stunned into silence.

Gelawezj laughed. 'We live in different times now,' she reassured them. 'Women are no longer expected to marry without getting to know their partner and there is more room for personal choices. But with this newfound freedom, we women have an extra responsibility. The responsibility of choosing.

'But don't you want to be conquered? Courted! A real man doesn't just wait patiently for you to make a choice,' the maid replied.

'But how should one choose?' the princess asked.

'A woman's choice is not one of weighing and judging. It is a choice of the heart. The first thing you must understand, my dear, is that men only grow up when they devote their heart to a woman. Before that, and for some that will last their entire lives, they remain like children chasing each other around the playground. Only with larger consequences.'

Runak reacted horrified. 'But I don't want to be mothering him, mom. I find this whole plan increasingly terrible by the minute.'

'The worst thing you can do to your man is mother him, my dear daughter,' the queen said with a smile. 'You will not understand these words yet but remember them well. Choose a man who stands with open arms in the storm of your love. Choose a man who will never hinder the flow of your heart. Choose a man who places you on a pedestal but never lets you walk over him, who worships you as lovingly as he contradicts you. Many women smother their fire to avoid burning the man they love. In doing so, they harm their longing to be loved and hinder their husband's necessary growth.'

The maid paused her brushing to wipe away a tear. The young woman had felt her own constrained heart in the queen's words – a heart that could burn as the sun and be as gentle as a warm bath. She had made herself smaller, hoping not to scare off the man she longed for, to avoid being too much. Only now did she feel the violence she had inflicted upon herself.

A person should first and foremost be loyal to their own heart. For it is in that heart where their fate lies. Only when they follow this heart and no other can they merge with another heart whose fate is intertwined with theirs. That realization manifested itself in her as a relief that washed away her doubts, like the sea washes away the sand.

In the following weeks, the princess was introduced to many young and old men who dared to try to win her love. On the king's council they limited themselves to three young men who were allowed to speak with the princess personally, after the initial meetings. 'The son of the Salahadins is intelligent and his family is well-disposed to us. He would help solidify a formidable alliance. The Qubads manage a strong line of warhorses. With them by our side, we would double our military strength. But the Xurmals are wealthy and sharp traders and hold many important posts.'

Runak, unfamiliar as she was in this area, relied on her father's knowledge and conviction. The first two were eloquent and valiant. They missed no opportunity to sing praises of her beauty. They would give her the world to win her favor. Every evening, as they were traveling to the palace, they had longed more fervently to see the princess and once in her presence, they were blinded by her beauty and graceful appearance, or so they claimed, each in their own extravagant way.

'Too tiresome,' the princess sighed to her maids. 'Are they all this intense?'

Reluctantly, she began her meeting with Yaran Xurmal. Runak braced herself for yet another monologue upon meeting him, but he merely introduced himself with his name. Instead of relief, she felt disappointed. Apparently, she had taken some pleasure in the praises after all. Their conversation was timid but pleasant. Her conversation partner seemed more searching than determined. The topics were plain and of little importance, but at least it was an actual conversation.

'Yaran, why should I choose you as my husband?' she finally asked to move beyond the superficial.

He laughed. 'To be honest, princess, it's my father's wish that I marry you. Personally, I've never been interested in marriage. But he thinks it's an excellent opportunity to expand our family's influence. At least, that was what I thought until I saw your eyes shining during my reception.'

Yaran's compliment came unexpectedly and therefore broke through Runak's defenses. It was this unguardedness that tunneled its way to a dormant part of the princess, a part that felt safe because there was no performance being staged. Yaran simply laid bare his inner world and that world felt like a place where she could feel at home.

Runak's natural curiosity was piqued, accompanied by a small fire in her belly. 'And were you, like the others, also "overwhelmed by my stunning irises, brown like the bark of a tree at snowfall," Yaran?' she said teasingly.

They walked through the palace garden, where they remained in sight. The scent of jasmine and lilies accompanied them at every corner. He stopped and looked into her eyes for the first time during their conversation. 'No, I was overwhelmed by your gaze.'

Runak was startled by his directness. 'What do you mean?'

'You looked at us as if we were merely a steppingstone to something greater. Some grand play in which I have a role to fulfill.'

A day later, they got engaged and a week later, their wedding began. The extravagant celebration took over the whole city. For days, the streets were filled with magnificent music and dancing crowds. The finest food was available on every corner, day and night.

No one danced more exuberantly or enjoyed the celebration more than the two fathers, who were ecstatic about their children's choices. Yaran's father, because he couldn't imagine a more powerful ally than the king himself and the king, because the light of his life had fulfilled the conditions to succeed him by marrying someone from a respectable family. The exuberant joy of the two fathers did not escape the partygoers, and in hushed voices followed by roaring laughter, they were jokingly named 'the bearded brides.'

Agha Simko had also offered his sons, but despite his respectable position, they had not even been invited for a conversation with the princess. Simko was not only aggrieved by the immediate rejection of his sons but also because he had preferred to offer himself. Older, more experienced and head of the second most powerful clan, he was undoubtedly the best choice. With disdain, he watched a wedding where he should have been the guest of honor.

The newlywed couple sat timidly on their throne and tamely received all the well-wishers bearing gifts. An endless stream of people welcomed them into their new life, with a cheerfulness that neither of them could reciprocate. In all the chaos and uncertainty, at least they shared the same state of mind. They didn't know what to expect from this new chapter in their lives, but at least they didn't know together.

Runak and Yaran spent their entire honeymoon getting to know each other. No more than a seed had been planted before they married, the beginning of a loving relationship. The first moment of deepening came as they were enjoying the sunset together. After spending the day together, they rested in the gardens. The princess was enchanted by the sun illuminating the hazy peaks of Korek until they formed a warm color palette in the sky.

She turned to her husband and met his gaze. The sun illuminated the left side of his face, giving him a celestial hue. His eyes did not wander over her body but went straight through her, as if trying to glimpse the innermost parts of her soul. Under the warmth of his gaze, a desire kindled to feel the warmth of his embrace.

In the days that followed, they learned about each other's childhood, their dreams, and their fears. They lost themselves in long conversations and shared laughter that left their stomachs aching. They recognized so many similarities in their biographies that they began to believe they were mirror images of one another, with their differences turning into each other's complements.

On a certain night, when emotions ran higher than words could keep up with, they discovered each other's touch. Neither of them knew who touched the other's hand first. They only remembered the sudden spark that shot through them, but supported by their marital status, their hands rested on top of each other. The desire grew stronger, their eye contact deepened and the distance between their bodies shrank. Their lips found each other like estranged lovers, reunited after a long bout of loneliness. Her body was soft and welcoming, his held her firm and brought her into ecstasy. Their skin longed for each other and their limbs removed the cloth barriers between them. Before they knew it, they were lying on the bed, skin to skin, sunk into a world where nothing existed but the sensations of their bodies.

In the days and nights that followed, they came to know every inch of each other's bodies: the sensitive spots, the soft spots, the secret spots. They learned to bring each other pleasure with their sstares and hands, with their words, with their mouths. From the first touch, Yaran had noticed how her body responded to his advances, and feeling her open to deeper levels of pleasure drove him forward.

In a blind desire to experience what more was possible, he sought the edge of her comfort. The gentle yet determined perseverance of her husband kept the princess in a constant state of excitement. She discovered parts of herself she had never known before: a softer part, a part that longed to be safe in his embrace, but at the same time to be overwhelmed by his determination. She craved his confidence and allowed him into her body. And through her body into her heart. Their bodies melted together, and they felt what it meant to wholly receive one another. The nights were filled with a passionate desire, which, once quenched, gave way to a tender love.

On a certain night, a buried memory surfaced in Runak's mind. Long ago, she had met a boy by the Zab who spoke of things she did not understand. Hemin's words echoed in her head, but only now did she realize he and his beloved had experienced the same thing she was experiencing with Yaran.

She wept for the crime they had fallen victim to and for Hemin's loss. She wept for her cold demeanor toward a boy who didn't understand what he had discovered. She wept because he had no one to tell him that his love wasn't wrong but only the beginning of a perfect beauty.

Her newlywed husband, startled by the fear of having done something wrong, hurried to warm her in his arms. 'My love, I'm sorry I've hurt you. Tell me what I've done.' He wiped the tears from her face and saw in her eyes that the love was still intact.

'You could never hurt me,' Runak replied.

'What is it, then, that torments you, my love?'

She looked at her husband and felt her love growing by the second. Even in her sorrow, he held her with the same tenderness in his gaze. 'We must never forget that our love doesn't revolve around pleasure or enjoyment. This love demands something of us. I don't know yet what, but whatever it is, we must become worthy of it.

16

The scouts had returned. Brave horsemen had ventured into the unknown terrain beyond Zagros to explore. There, they learned that the tyrant Zahhak still ruled over the land of their ancestors, even after a thousand years. But no tyrant can rule unopposed forever. Where despots make victims of righteous men, the trampled unite in ever-growing numbers.

This revolt found its origin in a father for whom the sorrow of doing nothing was greater than the pain that awaited him as a rebel. Kawa was a blacksmith who worked in Zahhak's palace. Day in and day out, he labored in the searing heat to create the finest tools and weapons. But no matter how hard he worked, how refined his craft became and how much Zahhak benefitted from his work, Kawa could not protect his family from the blind greed of the king. Six of his children had already been sacrificed to the king's insatiable hunger and when his last child was called for, Kawa became the first in a thousand years to dare defy the king's will. He tore off his charred apron in the king's hall and made it into a flag. Marching through the streets, he quickly gathered a small following. He traveled through the villages and eventually into the mountains. Everywhere he went, his ranks grew, for no place was without tales of sorrow and loss, waiting like seeds in the winter soil for the spring.

'Your majesty, Zahhak's reach is as gruesome as it is vast. That's why Kawa will find allies wherever he goes. And as children of the same line of victims, they request us to join them in this holy war.'

The court was filled with people who had come to hear the scouts' report. Seated on the throne was their new leader, Queen

Runak. She was only a few years older, but in a short time she had made the role her own. Her face had outgrown the childlike innocence, and she had shed her naivety.

The queen rose with her chin held high. 'Bring the message to Kawa the blacksmith that they will find allies in our united forces.'

The hall erupted in proud applause for their queen.

She waited for the commotion to settle. 'Go and deliver this message to all the clans. Tell them that the day when we avenge ourselves and finally live in freedom is soon at hand.'

The armed forces were, first and foremost, loyal to their local chieftains. In the past, these clans would, depending on the circumstances, form alliances or wage war against one another. Even King Sherwan could not rely on blind loyalty but would have to negotiate or if necessary, fight to maintain his position. But those age-old rivalries were slowly but surely crumbling. The discovery of their shared history was reason enough to bury the conflicts and pledge their weapons to the new queen.

Troops from all layers of the populace and from every clan had gathered to embark on the long journey, a journey that would take them beyond the Zagros. With anticipation, this gathered army awaited their queen's speech.

Runak hesitated. She had quickly mastered the theater of the court, but she had never seen a battlefield, nor did she know how to inspire troops for battle. The sheer number of warriors before her was intimidating. The sound of thousands of clanking armors and weapons pulled her out of her focus.

The troops carried weapons and armor that reflected their local tradition, so that one could see from a glance where another hailed from. Only the female soldiers shared a custom that was present across all clans. Each of them carried a small, razor-sharp dagger hidden under a piece of cloth under their dominant wrist. This dagger was not meant for the enemy, though many of them would lose their lives to it before it was used for its intended purpose. These daggers were meant to ensure they would not lose their honor were they to ever fall into enemy hands.

'My soldiers, prepare yourselves!' Runak tried to sound loud, but her voice ricocheted off all the clanging armor and her words disappeared in the open field.

Unrest spread among the ranks.

From one of the flanks, a large man on horseback emerged and presented himself to the assembly. Agha Simko had arrived. For men like Simko, women can only be one of two things: a trophy to be won or an obstacle to be destroyed. And Runak had made the first option impossible.

'Majesty, we are honored to serve you and eagerly await your encouragement. Our success rests on your shoulders.'

The queen attempted to respond firmly, but before she could speak her words, he interrupted her. 'Your Majesty, no ruler can be successful without a champion. Even your reign, wise and powerful as you are, cannot escape fate.'

He switched his gaze with studied regularity from Runak to the troops. 'If we set out without a champion, our mission will be in danger.' He paused before continuing his speech to give doubt enough opportunity to take root.

'Your sly tongue will not go unchecked today, Agha Simko,' Rezan retorted, skilled in detecting political motives. His horse moved toward the agha, neighing and pawing at the ground, as if unsettled by the underlying tension. 'Your opportunistic attempts to undermine Queen Runak will not go unnoticed.'

Two of Simko's men stepped forward, prompting the agha to feel compelled to answer Rezan's challenge. He could not afford to allow any doubts to arise about his manliness. 'Is this how the youth show respect to their elders these days?'

Some of Rezan's men now joined him as well. Slowly, two groups began to form, consisting of Rezan's and Simko's troops, who were ready to defend the honor of their leader. Rezan spat on the ground in front of Simko's feet.

'Careful, boy. Respect for elders is a privilege you don't want to abandon on the battlefield,' the agha said as he kept his prancing warhorse in check.

'And otherwise, I'll carve the respect into you so you won't forget,' one of Simko's men added with his hand on the hilt of his dagger.

All the men wrapped their hands around their hilts, ready to draw their weapons. The assembled army were on the verge of turning into an internal conflict before they had even marched a single step.

Yet, Rezan could not let such a threat pass unanswered. With an icy voice he responded, 'If you are a man, you'll say that again, you little runt.'

The horses grew more restless, and dust was kicked up by their stationary stomping. The voices grew louder and at the same time, the conversation became harder for the troops outside the circle to follow. The animosity had erupted like a storm, seemingly out of nothing and threatened to tear apart the unity of the soldiers and turn them into enemies.

Before the situation could escalate further, all heads turned at the resonant sound of iron clashing against iron. They saw a black horse and a figure galloping towards them from the direction of the sun. The horse was adorned with dazzling gold ornaments and its pounding hooves echoed like the sound of war drums. Before they recognized Akam, they recognized the black stature as the unwieldy Raksh, the horse that answered to but one rider. Raksh charged down the hill in a cloud of dust that reflected his shadow as large as he was in the minds of his comrades. On his back, he carried the one champion respected among all the warriors.

It had been Hanar who convinced Akam to put his armor back on and offer himself to the new queen. After his release, she tended to him with the greatest care. She sat by his bed until all his wounds had healed, but it soon became clear that his injuries were deeper than just the flesh. Akam had put away his armor. He found solace in the time spent with his wife and daughter, the two people that mattered most to him.

Hanar enjoyed finally having him all to herself. The fear the weeks of waiting were a thing of the past. For a while, they lived in blissful unity, the three of them. A lost dream, one that neither of them had dared to envision, became reality at last.

Until the call for warriors came and Akam declined. Hanar heard the fear in his voice as he sent the envoys away. Choosing to stay with his family in the light of such an appeal muffled his fire and made him complacent. The attention for his daughter became slightly less, but enough for Hanar to notice. And when they made love, she only felt his body, because he had to suppress his heart to remain in the safety of her embrace. She felt an unbridled power in him ready to burst, but he contained it with all he had. As if the fortitude that loved her whole was the same one calling him to battle.

One night, as they lay beside each other, Akam gently traced his fingers over her skin. Thoughtful, soft, as he always did and she would feel his love seeping through his fingertips into her skin, finding its way to her heart, where she kept his heart safe with care. But tonight, all she felt was gliding fingers. Just skin on skin, flesh on flesh.

'Where are you, Akam?' she whispered softly, as only lovers speak to each other.

He hesitated and stopped his caresses. 'With you, my love. Where I've always wanted to be.' He answered calmly, but his voice betrayed his unwillingness to reveal his pain.

Hanar shook her head. She already knew what it was that tormented him, but she longed for his presence, for him to not look away from his inner self and not withhold the stirring of his soul from her. 'You've never been as far away as you are now. At times, I've waited weeks for your return. I tried for months to find you in your cell, in vain, not knowing whether you would ever come back. But even in that solitude, you were closer to me than you are now. Why can't I feel you, Akam? Why do you close your heart to me?'

Silence filled the room like a wall between two lovers. Akam's response had a long path to traverse. He struggled to free it. His beloved waited patiently for his victory. She waited in the lush forest that once had been a barren tundra until her warrior found his way to her. Her beating heart no longer cried for help. It beat in unison with the heart that had been gifted to her as if to say, find me, my love, for every fear you withhold from me is a departure from yourself. Speak what you fear, for to close yourself off from me is to close off from yourself.

Hanar's touch and patience showed Akam the way through every tree and hill. Her heartbeat made the trees beckon him towards her.

'I'm afraid to lose you,' he finally said with teary eyes.

Hanar said nothing, for she knew there was more he had to say.

'When I was alone in that cell, all I could do was think of you. And there, I realized I left you alone for people who would betray me at the slightest whim. How could I ever risk losing you again?'

She stroked his hair. With his pain laid bare, he was more beautiful to her than ever, braver than in any battle. 'Because you don't risk your life for them, Akam. You risk your life for us. Your mission in this life is to protect our queen. Only by staying true to your mission can our love bloom. In trying to hold onto our little paradise, you are extinguishing the fire that makes our love possible.'

Hanar's words were sharper than any sword, more accurate than all the archers. Simply by speaking, she could penetrate the thickest armor and bring the mightiest man to his knees.

'Akam, you gifted me your heart long ago. Nothing in this world can harm it as long as it's with me. But your body has always belonged to the world. I'm grateful to her for every minute I have been given with you, but your fire must burn. Your fire must light up the darkness, or you will smother the flames, and we will suffocate in your smoke.'

With the fanned fire raging through his body, Akam galloped past the troops. With his sword held high, accompanied by the thunderous drum of Raksh' hooves, his roar ignited the fighting spirit of all the soldiers. His shout came from the underworld and caused all hearts to tremble. Akam's battle cry echoed like a storm, more powerful than the storm threatening to tear them apart.

They reacted like they were possessed and felt compelled to answer his call with the same passion, as if to prevent the ground beneath their feet from tearing apart. Only with thousands together could they match his battle fervor and create a united storm of passion, fighting spirit, and unity.

Without words, solely with his ferocity, solely with his strength and fire, Akam had turned a collection of soldiers into an army. They were bound together by their reverence for the man they would follow without hesitation to face death.

The queen, reassured, could answer Agha Simko. 'Your concerns are honorable, but unfounded. As you can see, our champion is already present.'

17

The army faced a grueling journey ahead. They would enter the Zagros Mountain range via Korek and travel eastward through the ancient cedar forests. From the top of Qandil's towering peak, they would cross over to the land of their ancestors. From there, they would be in uncharted territory.

For generations, they had ignored that other side while staying within the safety of the familiar. They shielded themselves from their dark origins. But what had brought their ancestors to the Zagros could not be denied. The hard-to-cross mountain range was now nothing more than a veil separating them from the darkness that they had to overcome to be free: Zahhak.

The Zagros was no longer that barren landscape Runak knew from her visit years ago. The once bleak paths were now covered with soft grass. There was plenty of shade from lush fauna to keep cool. Water was regularly replenished at small, often hidden springs, where it was clear and brisk, just as her mother had described to her long ago. How different could the same path be, she thought.

After the crossing at Qandil, they continued until the next mountain peak: Mamand Aqa. Here, for the first time, they could look out over the foreign land. It was clear something terrible awaited them; a dark cloud loomed over the landscape, where no ray of sunlight could reach the ground.

'It's always like this, Your Majesty. Season after season,' said one of the scouts.

'Is it safe to enter?' Yaran asked.

'Yes, my lord. I cannot imagine what it must be like to live in that darkness, but we made it out without a scratch.'

With every step down the mountain, the vegetation grew sparser and more sorrowful. The closer they came to the cloud, the more everything seemed covered in a layer of soot. Eventually, they entered the cloud itself and found themselves in a place where nothing grew. An icy silence hung in the air, unbroken even by the wind. Once at the foot of the mountain, the scouts led them to the camp of the blacksmith turned rebel.

Kawa was a large man with a gleaming bald head, as if it had been polished for the occasion. His face was covered by a thick beard and a warm smile. Welcome, esteemed guests! We are honored and delighted to finally receive the renowned Kurds.'

His guests looked at each other in surprise. Kurds?

'Among them, "Kurd" means something like a mountain dweller or nomad, Your Majesty,' a scout explained.

'And we Kurds are honored to go into battle alongside a brave man as yourself, Kawa,' Runak said.

Kurd. It became a title they would wear with pride, uniting them under a single common name. Until now, the Kurds had only known each other as members of their respective clans. It was only in their encounter with outsiders that they received a collective name for the first time, and it was their queen's reaction that granted the label legitimacy.

The Kurds and Kawa's troops spent weeks training together, learning to complement each other in battle. Kawa's troops were well-organized and fought as a single unit. The Kurds were fierce and formidable archers, both on horseback and on foot. Before long, they found strength in each other's advantage and complemented each other where needed.

Kawa's troops needed more time to get used to the female warriors among the Kurds, who were every bit as formidable as their male counterparts. The Kurdish men had learned from a young age not to approach these women carelessly, the way a deer might be approached by a hungry predator. Kawa's men would soon learn the same lesson, but not without the cost of a few crooked noses and wounded egos. Shared hardship, once reconciled, fosters brotherhood.

The leaders occupied themselves with devising a plan to defeat Zahhak.

'The city walls of Hashrud, Zahhak's home, rise high like an eagle and are as thick as elephant's hide. Even the Kurdish archers cannot shoot over them,' said one of Kawa's generals. 'Even with our combined forces, we have to admit to not having the strength to successfully lay siege to the city.'

The candlelight in the main tent cast a shadow on the faces of those present, each of them racking their mind on how to defeat their greatest nightmare.

'We'll lure him out,' Yaran said. 'On open ground, our swift riders can surround his troops while Kawa's forces keep them occupied.'

'And why would Zahhak leave the safety of his fortress?' another retorted.

Yaran crossed his arms. 'We encircle the city and block all supply routes. They will only last so long without fresh supplies. They'll have to choose between attacking quickly or risking a future battle when their troops are starving and demoralized.'

Now, those present responded enthusiastically to Yaran's proposal. As a merchant, he knew how dependent a city was on constant supplies and how to cripple one's enemy without direct combat.

'And the surrounding villages would continue to supply us without issue.' The plan was strengthened by someone else.

The enthusiasm grew. Without lacking anything themselves, they could suffocate Zahhak's troops. But Kawa did not rejoice. His face only grew more concerned, and his heavy voice cut through the excited chatter. 'This plan would be excellent, if only we were not facing a devil.'

His eyes stared into the burning candle, as if a terrible vision in the dancing flames had taken hold of him. Beside him stood his ox-headed axe, a weapon forged by his own hand, which he now increasingly leaned on. 'I saw it with my own eyes the day I confronted him; the monster Zahhak has become a sight I prefer to not put into words. The most important thing is that he has grotesque wings. If we surround him, he can bombard the villages from the sky, where we cannot reach him. And he would fly away effortlessly the moment the ground beneath his feet became too hot.'

The sparkling eyes of the others turned glassy, as if the dancing flames had seized them as well. Victory seemed further away than ever.

'Then we must settle the battle in a single swift strike,' Runak said. 'If I understand correctly, Zahhak rules through fear. His soldiers will not continue fighting if the source of their fear is gone. We will cut off the head of the snake and not let ourselves be distracted by the rest of its body.'

She had learned what influence she could have on her subjects. As her power and legitimacy grew, she also realized that her mere presence instilled fear in them; servants worked harder, nobles spoke more eloquently, and soldiers stood straighter the moment she entered the room. And if fear was her shadow, then inspiration would be her gift. Her steadfastness would inspire a solution.

'I once had an older brother,' said one of Kawa's followers, breaking the silence. 'As long as I can remember, he would talk about a tunnel he was digging. Day in, day out, he worked on it in secret. It was supposed to be a way out, he told me, but I never dared to accompany him. One day he walked out of the door and never came back.'

While all eyes were anxiously fixed on him, he suddenly stopped and fell into silence. He was the only one still captivated by that candle. He had always thought that his brother must have been captured or executed, but after hearing the Kurdish queen's resoluteness, he dared to dream of another possibility.

'And!?' shouted one of Kawa's men in tense anticipation.

The man was pulled out of his trance. 'And, what?'

Kawa nearly fell off his chair. 'The tunnel! Have you seen the tunnel?'

'No, I never had the courage to go there.'

'But you know where it should be?' Yaran interjected.

'Yes!'

That was all they needed to shape the plan. They would use the tunnel to sneak into the city with a small group. Inside, part of the group would continue to the palace, while another would open the gates so the army could wreak havoc in the city.

'Excellent. Kawa, Akam, Yaran, ten of our best warriors, and I will confront Zahhak,' Runak said.

'Your Majesty, you cannot place yourself in danger,' the man protested.

'Queen Runak, as my guest, I cannot allow you to put yourself in danger,' said Kawa.

The rest of those present agreed with them. Little had changed since the day the magician and architect stood in her room. Even now, most still saw her as a porcelain ornament that had to be handled with care. Only Yaran and Akam knew it was pointless to try to change the queen's mind. They remained silent and calmly awaited her next words.

Her will was like an anchor, her decisions unwavering. 'I will witness Zahhak with my own eyes,' was the queen's response and like a squall, she extinguished all opposition.

'As you wish, Queen Runak. With that group, we will proceed, but we will need a platoon to secure the path through the city for them.'

Kawa left the details to his subordinates and requested the queen to accompany him. Some matters are meant only for ears atop the chain of command.

They walked through the camp, where campfires burned and laughter with songs filled the air. Everywhere they passed, the liveliness quieted into solemn tributes or respectful greetings.

'Your reign is even more impressive than your army, Your Majesty,' Kawa said.

'Mine was bestowed upon me, without any merit of my own. Yours, on the other hand, is entirely your own achievement,'

Runak replied, knowing that in politics, compliments often are followed by requests.

Kawa gestured toward a slope and let the queen go ahead. 'I am merely a follower, Your Majesty.'

'How does a simple follower gain so many followers of his own?'

'Because it is not people that I follow. I follow a sacred angel, Sarush. He appeared in my dreams and commanded me to rise up in rebellion. That is why I'm convinced that victory will be ours, for we carry out a divine duty.'

I've seen heaven and it was empty. Runak did not say it, knowing that spoken words echo in reality and take on a life of their own.

Kawa followed her up the slope, which grew steeper and rockier. 'And once our victory is achieved, will the Kurds then return to their true king, Your Majesty?'

Runak turned around and looked down on Kawa. 'And who is that king, dear Kawa?'

He stopped and, while panting, pointed eastward. 'On Mount Alborz, he awaits our victory. A young child, chosen by Sarush himself as the rightful king. He is called Fereydun.'

Runak walked on to the edge of the rock. She gazed over at the troops and saw that both her followers and Kawa's stood together in groups. Despite a thousand years of separation, they had grown fond of each other surprisingly quickly.

Kawa joined her side.

'The Kurds have a queen and beside her a wise king, dear Kawa. For many generations, we have built our kingdom and shaped our own rule. There is only one thing that still binds us in fear to a past that none of us remember, and that's why after our victory we will become cherished allies.'

The Kurds had not returned; they were on an expedition, Kawa realized. 'And every king dreams of allies like yourself, Your Majesty.' He gave a slight bow with his hand on his chest. 'There is one more thing that the angel commanded me to do. That is to chain Zahhak alive beneath Mount Damavand.'

Runak wondered whether this had been Kawa's intention all along. In truth, he was asking her to spare Zahhak's life. Perhaps he was as formidable a politician as he was a rebel. Runak looked up at the full moon. Years ago, she had looked down from there, towards the earth. She saw herself upside down, hanging from the rock like a bat clinging to a wall, gazing down at the moon. 'Breaking the chains of the past or obeying a heavenly authority. Is that the choice you're asking me to make, Kawa?'

18

The infiltration platoon crept in the dead of night toward the place where the tunnel should be. A skillfully concealed crevice near the imposing city walls awaited them. Like a splinter that can pierce the thickest skin, it remained there as a reminder that no barrier can withstand the desire for freedom. Thanks to that desire, hidden in the shadows, they entered the city unnoticed.

A dismal silence reigned on that unrelenting night. The trembling bodies of fearful parents echoed off the city walls in a stifling stillness. They had entered the opening in groups of five and secured the surroundings. Without as much as a peep, the platoon reduced passing guards and civilians to lifeless corpses; they could not afford to risk being discovered.

Kawa, Yaran, Runak, Akam, and ten other fighters were the last to enter and immediately moved through the cleared street towards the palace that stood out against the dark sky. They passed their comrades and walked over the blood of their victims, with eyes fixated on their target.

A short time later, they heard the first sounds of unrest as the guards realized the gates had been breached. The streets filled with the echoes of clashing steel, screams, and the cracking of bones. Centuries of resentment, passed down from generation to generation, found its echo in the piercing of Zahhak's pawns. The lucky ones died quickly; others felt the cold iron penetrate their bodies multiple times before they took their last breath. The Kurds and Kawa's troops slayed their way through the streets of the city to draw all attention away from the small group on whom they had pinned their hopes.

In the palace as well, soldiers sprang to their feet, rushing toward the battle. The heroes used the chaos to slip past them, entering with even less resistance ahead. Kawa knew the way and the few remaining guards were quickly neutralized. Before anyone could notice the bodies, they had already turned down another corridor.

The small group guarding the entrance to the throne room met the same fate. Three were struck by arrows in the neck and the other three in a short swordfight. They pushed the doors open and entered the hall. They found the king in his most monstrous form. Zahhak was feasting on a decapitated child's body, while the two snakes fought over children's heads and a second corpse.

The pieces of flesh and brain tissue still hung from Zahhak's mouth as he looked up. 'Kawa, my servant. You've returned and brought my lost children with you,' said the monstrosity in a faint gurgling voice.

After a thousand years of cannibalism and mingling with the snakes, Zahhak's human form had twisted into a reptilian monstrosity. The snakes had grown into anacondas and two horrific wings had sprouted from his back. His body was covered in spiky scales and with each breath, he absorbed the little light in the room and exhaled suffocating smoke. The snakes on his shoulders coiled around him, protecting their host.

Beside him stood two demonic associates. They were just as monstrous, and each had burning eyes whose embers struck out and branded their faces at all moments, keeping them in a state of constant fury. Once humans, they were previous heroes who had been transformed into dews by dark magic. With their enormous weapons, they stood in front of their king.

'Your end is near. The saved children have grown into an army that will bring your reign to its fall,' Runak snarled at him.

Zahhak threw the child's body aside and let out a cold laugh. 'The cooks who thought they were heroes. It was only a matter of time before we figured it out. They were a fine dessert.' He licked his lips with his forked tongue as he looked Runak up and down. 'If I'd known they were hiding the most delicious children, we would have come looking for you as well.'

Yaran shot forward, unafraid of the monstrosities and headed straight for their master. He was stopped by the first dew's sword and saw Akam shoot past him, deftly evading the second dew. The dew facing Yaran was thrown off balance by Kawa's axe and the remaining soldiers surrounded the other.

Akam engaged in battle with the source of their misery, the shadow that also taunted him throughout his life. In the background, the battle cries of his comrades echoed, entangled in a fight between life and death. He was assured of backup and swung his sword.

Zahhak's skin was thick, and the metal bounced off his scales. 'With that pitiful piece of iron, you dare battle with the lord and master of all realms of this world?' he mockingly shouted.

The snakes tried to bite Akam. Their speed and strength were hard to match, but tirelessly, Akam kept dodging each strike. When the snakes couldn't reach him, they spat venom his way, which burned holes in the ground and turned the throne room into an unpredictable space with increasingly more pitfalls.

'Like a fly, you try to avoid me, but my power is unstoppable!' Zahhak screamed.

With each dodge, Akam's movements grew calmer, more methodical, and smaller. As Zahhak's snake continued to lash out furiously, Akam maneuvered so that his prey was cornered between him and the wall.

A gleam in those eyes of immeasurable darkness was the signal for Akam to launch his spear. Before the venom could be spat, the spear pinned the reptile to the wall through its soft palate. The already produced venom burned a hole in its own mouth, as Zahhak screamed in pain.

Akam had shot forward, knowing his plan would succeed. He seized the moment to cut the snake in two through its gaping mouth with his sword, causing the lower jaw to fall to the ground, while the upper remained dangling from his spear.

Suddenly, he felt a sharp pain in his neck.

Zahhak's grimace turned into a grin. 'You didn't think this little scratch would bring down the great and immortal Zahhak, did you?'

Out of the corner of his eye, Akam saw the same gleam in the other snake's eyes, ready to bite through his neck. Before the creature had a chance, Zahhak was struck by Kawa's ox-head axe. The crack of bone and metal echoed through the room and ushered in an end.

All looked up from their fight and met the eyes of their comrades. A silent triumph filled the bloodstained room. The sparks in the eyes of the dews had been extinguished and their bodies lay motionless on the ground, surrounded by mangled human corpses. But there was no time for mourning for all eyes were fearfully fixed on the heavily bleeding Akam.

Zahhak's back was broken, and he lay helpless on the ground, his snakes equally motionless. One lay beside the kneeling Akam, while the other hung torn open, dangling from the wall.

Runak rushed to Akam and caught his head in her lap just before it hit the ground. Blood poured from his neck and stained her garments red. He tried to speak, but no words came out. The snake had sunk its teeth into his throat and torn it away as it fell to the ground.

Akam's eyes widened in panic as his comrades seemed unable to understand his words. A single tear reached the warrior's cheek. It wasn't death that frightened him, but the fact that the final expression of his heart would never reach his beloved home.

'My champion, rest easy,' said his queen. She summoned the strength to articulate her words clearly through her grief. 'My champion. I know what you wish to speak of in your final moments. I see within you what your deepest desire has been, just as you saw it in me. My champion, my friend, I'm sorry. I'm sorry that I took you away to fight for a peace you will never know.'

The queen's tears mixed with the warrior's spilled blood. As if her tears not only diluted his blood but also his pain. Akam found peace in his final moments. His queen would ensure that his last thoughts of his wife and daughter would find their way home. Runak saw the same look in his eyes as on the first night when she had commanded him to accompany her, away from his wife and child. Even then, she had recognized the longing in him to send words of love back home. Akam welcomed the darkness, knowing there was nothing left for him to do and left life behind.

As if the world itself wept for the passing of a hero, rain poured through the many gaps in the palace. For a moment, the sound of falling droplets was the loudest sound, while the war cries outside the palace slowly faded into silence.

A thunderous laughter shattered the solemn silence. Zahhak coughed up blood as he reveled in Akam's death. 'No ruler shall triumph without a champion, he declared with smugness. 'So, it is written. And I know you do not have permission to end my life. With my healing powers I will soo...'

Before he could finish his sentence, the queen had driven Akam's sword through Zahhak's throat. Her bloodstained gaze was even sharper than her blade. 'Not in a thousand years will I allow this hall to receive more blood from the hero Akam than from the devil Zahhak.' She left the sword in his neck and watched as he slowly bled to death. A swift death was too merciful for him.

As Zahhak convulsed, clinging to life, Runak saw the terrified child who had wrapped an armor of magic and kingship around himself. In his quest for security, he had seized every opportunity to further dismantle his humanity. In his final moments, Zahhak had the chance to repent, to reflect upon the totality of his deeds as his end drew near and realize he had lived a despicable life. He had the chance to feel his fear and loneliness and experience a glimmer of freedom before the boundless depths embraced him. For a brief moment there was a chance, but in the last pair of eyes he saw, there was no room for his pain. In Runak's eyes, he saw only the world that had tormented him since childhood and in his last moments, he was as he lived: bitter and afraid, enraged and full of hate, without compassion for the suffering he had caused.

With his last bout of strength, he opened his jaws, and a snake shot from his mouth and sank its fangs into Runak's throat. No one could stop the creature and all watched in horror.

The queen did not flinch and kept her eyes locked on her enemy with the same unwavering determination.

Zahhak died as he had lived: cowardly and bitter.

With Zahhak's death, the snake also fell to the ground, and Runak's damp skin revealed her true form. The serpent scales she had received through Shahmaran's blood protected her from the bite.

Rays of light broke through and brought a heavenly warmth, as though the sun itself was congratulating them on the triumph of light over darkness. The warmth and peace filled their hearts, though it was a painful peace, the kind one experiences when all grief has left the body through tears. After a thousand years, the sun decided to shine once again upon the land and lit up the intoxicating smog. The soot vanished and revealed the starving earth beneath. The grass and withered flowers seemed frozen under the ash but came to life with the first rays of the sun.

People emerged from their homes without fear and the laughter of children returned to the streets after they were cleared of the slaughtered soldiers. The long night had come to an end and a new day had dawned.

19

'Your Majesty, you have honored us by fighting alongside us,' said Kawa. They stood facing each other at the open gates of Hashtrud.

'And you have honored us,' Runak replied. She gazed out over the liberated city and the blue sky. Soldiers passed by them, beginning their journey home.

'Will you not stay to await our king, Fereydun? He would be overjoyed to meet you,' Kawa asked.

Runak looked at the passing coffins, filled with the bodies of their fallen comrades, waiting to be reunited with their families. 'Though that would be a great honor, we must return our martyrs to their final resting place, back among their loved ones.'

Kawa nodded understandingly. 'I would offer every Kurdish martyr the highest tribute, but I know you would not accept that. You will have your own way of honoring them.'

'And how do you honor your martyrs?'

Kawa's eyes filled with pride. 'We bring them to the Tower of Silence, where they are taken up into nature once again by vultures, so that in death they may nourish others, just as they nourished us in life.'

Runak looked up at the sky, where birds indeed soared. Could Simurgh be flying up there somewhere?

'And you?' Kawa asked.

She turned to the procession of fallen comrades, as if weighing her thoughts, and then looked down before meeting Kawa's gaze. 'Our martyrs will shine one last time before being consumed by fire. The wind will carry their ashes across the world, where they will nourish the earth and create life in places we may never know.'

'Godspeed to you, Queen Runak.'

'Godspeed to you, Kawa the blacksmith. Know that you will always find allies beyond the Zagros.'

They nodded to one another and Runak joined the ranks of her army, her loyal husband by her side.

'My love, wouldn't it have been better to wait for Fereydun?'

'Why would we, Yaran?'

'A shift in power is not seldomly also a shift of alliances. Building a bond with this unknown king could be important.'

'Nothing is more important than paying our martyrs their final tribute. And besides, we are not finished yet. We still must prove ourselves worthy to love.'

Yaran gazed at his wife in awe. She still had that look. She gazed into the distance, as if something was hidden there, meant solely for her.

Wherever Runak's Kurds placed their feet, they brought spring with them. The victory over the long night was complete and the blooming nature honored them with every step they took. At the peak of Korek, they lit a fire to celebrate this day and mark their homecoming. Soon, a similar celebratory fire was kindled in every village across the land.

Akam's body was tended to with the utmost honor and enshrined as the hero who had struck down Zahhak. He lay atop the funeral pyre, surrounded by his fallen comrades. For the second time, a crowd had gathered around him, this time not to denounce but to honor him.

Hanar bore the terrible honor of sending his body into the next life. She carried no torch up the pyre, for she didn't need one. A single kiss was enough to ignite the fire to burn one final time.

Their daughter was old enough to understand that her father would not wake up again. She leaned her small body over him and buried her face in his neck, her tiny hands resting on his cheeks. Her tears soaked his beard as she begged him to open his eyes.

Hanar gathered her daughter in her arms and kissed her husband farewell.

'Welcome home, my love. The world has taken you back,' she whispered as the flames embraced him in their bosom.

Her tears evaporated in the rising flames and ascended alongside his ashes. She didn't cry for the loss of his life, for a man who gives his life to that which is good is never truly lost. Akam had given her everything she desired from a man. He had given himself fully to the world, and through that, to Hanar. Her tears were for the sorrow of her daughter, who would never know the safety of his shadow, a safety she would now one day have to learn to cultivate within herself.

Akam's life had been devoted to conquest, but the heart of a woman cannot be conquered. Though you were to move heaven and earth, you will not force her heart to open. Akam had realized this on that silent tundra. The only thing he could do was present an offer to her altar: his heart. And in that union, he learned that a woman's heart is no different from the world itself. She gives and takes as she pleases, and the people can do nothing other than accept their fate. His heart belonged to Hanar, his body to the world. Both found their home in his final resting place.

The Kurds danced around the roaring fire to honor the fallen heroes. They celebrated their life through their dance. Each of them had wrapped an arm around the person next to them, moving in an open circle around the pyre to the rhythm of the def and the dahol, guided by the melodies of the simsal and tembur.

Their dance symbolized their close-knit community, where no one stood alone and all together followed their leader. The one in front of the line set the pace and energy, holding the honor of rousing everyone up and letting the music carry them away. It was a carefree and unifying dance; a dance where it didn't matter whether you were man or woman, king or subject, family or stranger.

The dark king had been vanquished and the Kurds felt assured they had no more enemies. In the years that followed, respect and reverence for Runak rose to new heights.

The victory over Zahhak and Akam's martyrdom were, on the advice of former King Shwerwan, skillfully used to solidify Runak's position. This great warrior's history with the royal family was lavishly celebrated, without that one dark period where he was nearly executed by them ever being mentioned again.

The warriors who had fought against Zahhak were richly rewarded and glorified. If these warriors later attained positions of power within their clans, they were drawn even closer to the royal house to strengthen their loyalty to the crown.

'A powerful warlord or clan chief will be less inclined to openly challenge you if they stand close to you,' the old king had advised. Even though Sherwan had become nothing more than an advisor, it was no secret that no major decision was made without his approval.

Runak also became increasingly active in intervening in rising disputes between local leaders. As a mediator between parties, her influence grew even further, and she had a good excuse to station her most loyal troops and generals everywhere. The power that village elders, clan chiefs, and warlords had over their own territories slowly shifted toward the center, toward Runak.

She followed her father's advice where it aligned with her objectives, but she had her own plans. Runak had never forgotten Hemin. She learned that the duty to uphold the family's honor weighed heavily on all families. It was a burden that suffocated young girls before they could blossom and one that turned brothers and fathers into remorseless hangmen.

Despite enjoying many freedoms and the ability to gain positions of power, it was still an undeniable fact for young girls they could not escape: the degree of freedom in their lives was determined by the men of the family they were born into. And it was exactly this fact that Runak aimed to destroy. To be worthy of love, she had to make the love she had found possible for everyone. Only in freedom can love truly blossom.

When her influence reached far enough and her will prevailed in every village and city, she enacted a ban on families disciplining their children as they wished. Taking a life would no longer be the prerogative of a patriarch. 'From now on, your lives are subordinate to nothing less than the crown,' she had demanded. 'We are no longer a collection of abandoned children. We are the people that saved the world from darkness and as a united people, we have but one leader.'

It was the first decision she made without consulting her father. 'She's making a great mistake!' Sherwan sighed to his wife, Gelawezj. 'You can't forbid the local leaders from managing their own family matters.'

His wife watched as her husband paced the bedroom. 'Isn't it better that she has control over those areas?'

Sherwan stopped and looked at his wife in frustration. 'It's about balance. Certain traditions you can't take away from them without rebellion. If it doesn't happen today, it will be used against her tomorrow.'

'Have we not come this far because someone dared to break traditions in the first place?' His wife responded, referring to his own decision regarding the succession. 'Perhaps it is time you trust that her vision reaches out further than yours.'

He collapsed beside her on the bed and leaned on his legs. 'There is so much at stake, Gelawezj. You can't just ignore all of that for a clear conscience.'

As the love between Runak and Yaran grew, so did a new need: the need to materialize their life, to bring it into the world and see it grow. And so, they had four beautiful children, each the spitting image of their mother or father. And in those children, they saw their love take on a new form, independent of themselves.

The former king and queen looked on with wide eyes at their new grandchildren. Sherwan forgot all his worries about his former kingdom, as he, taken in by the playfulness of the new children, laughed and joked with the playful little ones. It was as if a fifth child had joined them.

Runak watched her children being showered with love by their grandparents, free from their fear for the future. She looked on with pleasure at the contrast to her own childhood, because she could see that her parents' love could finally flow without fear, finding its equal in the joy of her children.

When both her parents died, she felt the same bottomless pit open beneath her feet as the day she was separated from Akam. But this pit was even deeper, for it was her own roots that withered away forever. The roots that had kept her firmly in place, supported her, and to which she could turn for the wisdom of the ages.

Only then did she learn how to be in the world again and to nourish herself. She learned to grow her own roots and be the support for her surroundings so that she was no longer just a ruler but also a support and refuge.

20

Every light casts its own shadow. And in Runak's light, a dark shadow grew. After the victory over Zahhak, Agha Simko was the only one who found no peace. His distrust of the unknown stubbornly clung to his heart. He had entered Zahhak's palace just in time to witness the monster bleed to death and saw how mesmerized everyone was by Runak's presence. The first sunbeam fell upon her visage and reflected off her snakeskin into his eyes. In that moment, Simko saw his own human shortcomings and the subordinate role that would befall him in her shadow.

The queen's growing influence troubled him. Slowly but surely, she was amassing enough power to overthrow him with ease. What would become of his life's work if she, like so many before her, decided to seize all power? What would remain of his bloodline if she sought to eliminate any chance of revenge after taking over his city?

He made attempts to forge a secret alliance against her, but no one dared to discuss the possibility, fearing that her spies lurked everywhere. How could they even harm her while her powers made her inviolable?

To no avail, he tried to obtain those powers for himself. His spies lingered around the royal household, attempting to uncover the source of her magic, but they found no trace of the supernatural. He scoured the forests, searching for the magical tree where Simurgh nursed her young, hoping to steal her powers. Perhaps if he could separate the creature from her offspring, he could train them to obey him. But after months of searching, the only thing he found was a solitary walnut tree; no hidden world unfolding, no magical fruit, no chirping birds.

He tried to find Shahmaran to drink her blood and become invincible, just like the queen. But all he found in Shaneder were endless cave systems and damp hollows. Snakes, scorpions, rats, and other vermin were plentiful, but none showed any trace of magic.

The world was empty because he was empty. Within him lived no heart of flesh and blood that could feel along with the hearts of other beings. And so, the entire world appeared to him as a soulless place, as a dead place that had nothing to offer unless he wielded power over it.

The World speaks freely to open hearts but falls silent before closed ones. And now that another held power over him, he felt as though he had become one of the dead things of the world and no longer possessed a will of his own.

Runak's father had also been powerful, but he had always remained a man of flesh and blood. Sherwan had to show Simko due respect to avoid the risk of rebellion. But this new queen tore through traditions and his power base without batting an eyelid. Defeated and bitter, Simko withdrew and abandoned his hopes for more power.

One day, a vagabond appeared at his court. The hooded man had requested an audience to ask the agha for a favor. Simko allowed the visitor to enter, hoping for some distraction.

'O, great Agha Simko,' said the man. 'My gratitude is immense to be received at the court of such a great man. A man with a heart that knows no equal and an unbreakable will. You honor me with this audience.'

Simko was not in the mood to entertain fawning strangers for long. Despite this, he enjoyed being praised, even though it was clear the man wanted something from him. 'What is your request, stranger?' he asked flatly.

'Great Agha Simko, far and wide I search this world for worthy men. Men like you, who rise above all others. I seek them to bestow my gifts upon them. And here before me stands the worthiest of them all.'

Simko rested his head in his palm in boredom. 'Your flattery works better if you dare to show your face.'

The visitor removed his hood. A young boy with white skin and green eyes appeared. He resembled an animated statue, so smooth and even was his skin. Only the green eyes revealed the life behind the porcelain apparition.

'Long you have lived in the shadow of others, great agha. First under the arrogant Sherwan and now under the naive Runak. Is it not time to claim your rightful place as ruler over all people?'

Murmurs filled the hall. Such insults were not to be spoken without opposition.

Simko stood up from his chair. 'Do not speak such treacherous words in my presence, or I will have you removed!' he shouted, in a feigned attempt to mask his own cherished dreams of treason. This young man had exposed his desires, and that awakened something within him.

'You wear your fears as an emblem on your chest, my lord,' the visitor said calmly. 'We can speak earnestly in front of all present, for after our conversation, you will no longer have anything to fear.'

'Who are you?' Simko asked, betraying his growing interest.

'My lord, this World is nothing but the battleground between light and darkness. And I, Ahriman, wander through the hearts of men since the dawn of time, seeking those with enough darkness within to be worthy of my gift of power. Your heart, great Simko, is charred black like coal, an endless pit capable of devouring all the realms under the sun.' The visitor bowed before continuing. 'If you would so choose.'

Simko's defenses crumbled under Ahriman's promising words. The young man had exposed his fears and desires and at the same time offered him salvation. 'And how does one acquire this so-called power?' he asked mockingly, in yet another futile attempt to mask his desire for the truth behind the words as mere jest.

Ahriman smiled, for this was exactly the reaction he had hoped for. 'Permit me to whisper it into your ear, my lord.' He ignored Simko's mocking tone and treated his response as a serious request, for beneath the surface, that was precisely what it was.

The agha couldn't help but hope. He convinced himself there was no harm in hearing the boy out. It was merely an amusing tale from someone peddling sweet words, yet the mere promise of such power sparked a hope he couldn't look away from. Simko forgot the others in the hall and motioned for his guest to come closer as he sank back into his throne.

Ahriman walked with steady steps towards Simko. 'The power I speak of is not one of iron and blood. We both know that your greatest enemy cannot be felled by any sword, but there is another way for you to ensure your dominion over her.'

He stood beside Simko. The latter was bursting with desire and now couldn't resist leaning in closer.

Ahriman placed his mouth near to his ear. His hand shielded his lips so no one could read them.

The guests didn't see that he uttered no words. Instead, he blew black smoke into Simko's ear, accompanied by an icy chill. Slowly, the smoke spread through his body and turned all organs to soot. Once he was completely filled from within, the black smoke escaped through every cavity and pore until he was entirely concealed, vanishing like snow before the sun.

The smoke spread until the entire room was filled, while all the other guests fled. It escaped through windows and cracks. Soon the agha's villa was no longer visible.

He engulfed the houses and their flowerpots, descended upon the busy stalls, and smothered the lively atmosphere as people scrambled to hide. The smoke consumed the entire city, cascaded down the plateau, and spread even further until it engulfed the Gara forests, Rebin's village, the Zab, Hanar's home, and Queen Runak's city.

He burst through the palace gardens and the courtyard and invaded the throne room where he covered all its beauty and splendor with a thick layer of ash so that every color of Queen Runak was as charred as Simko's own intestines.

Within moments, the entire kingdom was covered by a black cloud that spread panic among its victims. The ash settled on the trees and suffocated them. He weighed down the bird's mid-flight until they plummeted like stones. He crept into every home and extinguished every hearth, leaving the inhabitants in the cold. He wormed his way into their cranium and mangled their thoughts into fear and resentment and made brothers see each other as demons, and sisters see each other as wenches. Parents saw their children as cattle and children viewed their parents as merciless slavers.

The panic led to fear and distrust and the shadow they thought they had eradicated broke through the doors of their consciousness and took control. The weak feared the strong, and the strong unleashed all their fury on the weak. And the greatest overlord of them all became Agha Simko. He smothered every opposition before it could take shape and manipulated each thought so he was seen as the savior.

Only Simko himself remained as a shining light of hope capable of driving away the monsters. Only he himself was allowed to be unconditionally loved in this new nightmare.

'Was there no other way?' Runak gazed out from Korek at her kingdom, now buried beneath the same black smoke she had once driven away years ago.

Next to her stood a familiar old man, with his white beard and turban. 'Agha Simko has given himself fully to the darkness and abandoned his humanity for power. There was nothing you could have done. If you had not fled your palace, you would have been consumed like everyone else, and all hope would have been lost.'

They turned around and walked back to the caravan with several guards, servants, Yaran, and their children. They had fled in time thanks to the warning from the man she had met years ago, the sage who was interrogating a crowd about courage. Suqrat was his name. He had met Rebin in his homeland, the land of voting, and had traveled with him to the Zagros.

Up close, he had witnessed Agha Simko's decline. And with each expedition Simko returned from, he saw how his face was more overtaken by a dark shadow. With Ahriman's arrival,

Suqrat knew the end was near. After years of conversations in that square, he decided it was time to visit the girl who had become queen, the girl in whom he had once seen a fearless curiosity.

'We must head toward Kawa,' said Yaran. He was holding their youngest child, with another one by his side. The two others were flipping stones to find creatures underneath.

Runak nodded complacently as she took the child in her arms and felt her little hands curl around her neck.

21

Runak's heart felt heavy. She couldn't leave her land behind and abandon her people to their fate.

Yaran wrapped an arm around her in the wagon. 'Simko will do everything he can to take your life and kill our children, to crush even the smallest seeds of hope that still exist. But as long as you live, those seeds will patiently wait for the moment they can bloom.'

'What is the point of even more bloodshed?' Runak said sorrowfully. Her father had entrusted her with pulling their people out of the cycle of violence, but it was her own power that had driven Agha Simko into darkness. Returning to overthrow Simko would only mean a shift in power with eventually the same outcome as today.

At that moment, she remembered a story from long ago about a people where everyone had an equal say. 'Wise Suqrat, in your homeland, does not everyone have an equal voice in decision-making?' Runak asked.

Suqrat sat across from her and sighed, as if reminded of an embarrassing past. 'Ah yes, even the most foolish citizen has as much to say as the wisest. It's a horror.'

'But isn't that the way to break this cycle of violence? To drive no one into the darkness, where their fears can twist their minds?'

Suqrat waved his hand through the air as if brushing the notion aside. 'And be certain that wisdom will be lost in the maelstrom of fools.'

Rank sank into her seat. 'Are we then doomed to choose between foolish rule or certain violence?'

'Your Majesty, why do you believe foolish rule will not lead to certain violence?' Suqrat replied.

'Why do you call it foolish to share power?' Runak asked. 'It might've spared us today's tragedy.'

Suqrat crossed his arms and remained silent for a moment. 'King Yaran,' he said at last. 'When you negotiate the price of your goods, do you let everyone participate in the decision-making, or will you have the most skilled negotiator take the lead?'

Yaran laughed. 'If we let everyone participate, we'd go bankrupt within months, Suqrat.'

'And you, Queen Runak. When your children cough or are wounded, will you let everyone weigh in on the treatment or will you entrust that to a doctor?'

'I would of course, leave that to a doctor,' Runak replied indignantly.

'And why do you do that?'

'Because they could become even sicker if they do not receive the correct treatment.'

Suqrat leaned his arm on the carriage window. 'In other words, through ignorance, you could needlessly harm your children or your ventures. And just as in trade and health you must entrust leadership to the wisest and most intelligent, so too you must do in governance.'

Runak and Yaran exchanged questioning glances.

Yaran stroked his chin. 'But in trade and in health, the goal is clear,' he said. 'I know I want to get the lowest price possible. But what should be the goal of a kingdom?'

'That is an excellent question, wise king,' Suqrat said and continued to look out the window without answering.

Runak looked for the second time from the Zagros at the land of Kawa. By now, Fereydun would have already been installed as king. How would he receive her? As a loyal ally or a convenient pawn in negotiations? Would she be welcomed as a heroine who brought down Zahhak or as a heretic who flouted a divine command? At the very least, she would enjoy Kawa's protection. His bond with the Kurds had been forged in blood spilled together, usually a durable alliance.

'Here, we are safe from Simko, my love,' said Yaran, sensing his wife's troubled heart. 'And in time, we will gather troops and influence to one day face the agha again.'

Runak had little hope for a battle with a favorable outcome, and courage sank in her shoes. 'Wise Suqrat, when we first met, you were discussing courage, weren't you?'

'Yes, your Majesty.'

'What was your final answer on what courage is?' Runak asked, gazing into the distance.

He shrugged. 'Oh, that's something we never came to a conclusion on. We kept circling back to how courage encompasses all virtues, but that, of course, is a definition of virtue itself, not courage.'

'It's always easier to determine what something is not than to determine what it is.'

'That's right, your Majesty. There are countless answers to what something is not, but only a single answer to what it is.'

'That's why I can say with certainty that hiding is not courageous. Take us to your homeland. I will witness that form of government myself and determine whether it is foolish or wise.'
They traveled via Korek to the mountaintop of Maslawk, from there to Samdi, Silo and finally Cudi. The Zagros seemed to show

them the way, each new peak like a beacon. That same Zagros had once been a bleak landscape to Runak, then an oasis, and now a guide. Was the Zagros so changeable, or was it herself?

From Cudi, it was time to leave the Zagros behind. It had protected them all this time from the agha's darkness, but that was all they could do there: stay safe.

One day, they reached the end of the land as well, where the water lapped in waves over the sand. Runak stepped out to admire the view. The horizon stretched endlessly, causing her eyes to lose their bearings and relax. Her thoughts became small and trivial in the presence of the infinite sea.

She stepped onto the beach and felt the warm sand tickle beneath her feet. The water was cold but refreshing. On that beach, with her feet in the water, the wind caressed her legs. The sand between her toes washed away with each wave and made room for new grains.

In the glimmer of the sun on the grains of sand and the churning foam, she saw the true nature of this exchange. The sea and the land were two lovers, intimately intertwined from the beginning of time. The sea danced around her lover. She pulled and pushed; she flooded him with her body.

He, in turn, stood firm against her whims, immovable in his love for her and received her as she was. When she surged against him, he responded lovingly. When she caressed him, he never refused. When she took more than her share, he exploded from the depths of his being to reclaim what was his.

They took from each other, and they did not exist without one another. They were two lovers in perfect harmony in the never-ending war of love.

Runak had never felt that the stable ground which she lived on was the arena of a perfect love game, too consumed by her own drama. The World, which gave so lovingly and to which everything returned, was itself a battle between two parts of the same whole.

Just as every breath rises and falls, so it is with everything. Waves rise and disappear back into the sea. Humans sprout from the ground like seedlings and return to the earth. Kingdoms, lovers, thoughts; all follow the same path.

Runak believed that by killing Zahhak, she banished the darkness, but the darkness is not a man; it is not something that can die. The sea cannot exist without the land, inhaling cannot exist without exhaling, and light cannot exist without darkness.

She looked up from the breaking waves further into the sea and saw her old, winged door appear. The red-legged partridge looked even more spectacular than she remembered. From the cracks, a black shadow slipped out, sending a shiver down her spine. The door slammed open with a bang. A massive black cloud escaped and completely engulfed her.

Without being able to see anything, she gasped for breath only to burst into coughing. She reached out around her for something to hold on to, but there was nothing. The smoke filled her lungs until she collapsed to her knees, coughing. Her life flashed before her eyes as she gasped for air.

Swallowed up by that darkness, there was nothing left to do but accept what was about to happen. She took a deep breath and allowed everything to unfold. At least in her final moment, she would understand who the shadow was that had been chasing her all along. 'Show yourself,' she said.

A small hand gently touched her leg. A wave of warmth shot through her body, and the suffocating sensation transformed into a deep sigh that blew the smoke away. A tiny Runak stood before her, with arms wrapped around the hips of the larger Runak.

The weight of realization permeated through her. The shadow that she and her people had so anxiously tried to keep out had never been Zahhak. It was the little child within themselves that they had forgotten. The child who, before it ever had a chance, was sent into the mountains and forced to fend for itself. That child had repeated the same pattern for generations, hoping to finally be seen.

It had never been a bandit banging at the door. It was the child within themselves, clawing and begging to be let in, to be with them in the safety of their home, to not forget what they once dreamed of as children, to honor the pain they had endured. Left in the cold, that pleading child became bitter and distrustful, and when the opportunity arose, it manifested itself in the form of fear. And with that fear, it drove them to anger, conflict, and subjugation, hoping to find the safety that could only be found within their own hearts.

Runak wrapped her arms around herself. 'Thank you for never leaving me all these years, little Runak. I am sorry I never let you in, but I have finally found you, and I will never let you go again.'

She took the hand of her younger self and stood up to see her own children. Her beautiful children, who carried the same light within them. They were perfect little beings, with their laughter always in full bloom and their cries filled with emotion. Every emotion was pure and uncalculated, for they had not yet learned to mask their hearts.

Slowly but surely, the events in their lives would tunnel their way into those open hearts, leaving their mark behind. They would erect walls to protect the wounded parts. And little by little, they would become full-fledged individuals that would need to embark on their own quest back to their true selves, the same quest that Runak had to endure. The quest was only completed when she lost everything she had built.

Once, she had longed for nothing more than for the palace to disappear into darkness so that she would be free. But it was now clear to her what her purpose in life truly was, what her exhalation would be, for she had already found her freedom. In reconciling with the past and claiming the future, Runak had become free.

Courage is to heed the calling of your soul. To follow it, no matter which mountain or sea it leads you to. On that day, with feet between sand and sea, with the sun on her face, Runak heard her true calling for the first time. She did not know how light could exist in harmony with the darkness. She didn't know how to end the cycle of violence and the subjugation of the weak by the strong. But just as her parents believed in her, she believed in her children. The suffocating feeling from her childhood was her parents' hope that Runak would go further than they did, that she would right what they couldn't. Now it was her turn to pass that hope onto her children.

She would become the fertile ground in which they could take root, where they could grow big and become strong. Runak would dedicate her life to these four souls so that they would never close their hearts to their deepest selves. So that they would not forget their ancestors, so that they would not be driven by fear, so that they would one day claim their future. So that, when the child within them would finally knock on the door of their hearts after many years, they would not send it away as a stranger or leave it out in the cold. So that they would never be corrupted by the darkness because they were living in fear.

The World would one day demand her life back, demand her children back. And even the immeasurable Zagros would be powerless when it is swallowed into her bosom, and ultimately every sign of the drama of the Kurds would be swept away. But until that time, she still had a role to fulfill.

Runak's calling was to protect the light in her children's hearts and, when the time was right, to help them let their light shine. For one day, they would return to Kurdistan, those four beautiful children, Bakur, Bashur, Rojhelat, and Rojava, and they would fulfill the triumph of light over darkness as the children of the Zagros.

Afterword

There are few things worse than opening a book you've been looking forward to, only to be confronted by a foreword spanning multiple pages. As if you must first sit through a lecture before you're allowed to enjoy yourself. Hence, this afterword.

Around 2019, a new interest began to grow in me for the origins and history of the Kurds. For reasons I can no longer recall, I decided to search for those origins in stories and myths. I believed I might find a worldview or moral code that could be primordially Kurdish. That was, in short, a naïve undertaking.

Yet, even if a demarcated origin remains elusive, that doesn't mean there isn't a distinctive story to be told. And as I delved into the tales of Simurgh, Shahmaran, and Zahhak, combined with my own experiences and the psycho-political analyses of the Kurds by my father, Azad Qazaz, a new idea began to take shape. But it was no more than an idea at that time.

As cliché as it may sound, it wasn't until after a failed relationship that I dedicated myself to what I knew I should be doing but out of fear didn't dare: writing this story. It took me ten days to write half of this book, though at times it seemed to be writing itself. And it took nine months to finish the first draft of the manuscript. And it took another nine months before it was ready to print.

A work of art, and I include works of literature in that, should be able to stand on its own. Once it's finished, the author becomes just one of, hopefully, many readers. Just as a parent has no right to decide how their child should live, an author has no right to dictate how their work should be interpreted. Authors who wish to convey a one-sided message would be better off writing an essay.

I also wanted to avoid a foreword to prevent the reader from wondering what I might have meant in certain places. Far more important is it to ask yourself, or feel, what happens within you while reading the story. It's not as though everything was written with a preconceived intention either. Some elements only became clear to me after writing, meaning the author has to interpret the work just like any other reader.

Still, there were some things I had in mind while writing that might be interesting for the reader to know. First, I wanted to write a story that could resonate with anybody, regardless of background or beliefs. At the same time, I hoped that if you were indeed a Kurd, you would find a second layer of recognition as a reference to our shared culture. Some scenes, for example, were perceived as alienating by non-Kurdish test readers, and that was precisely the intention.

This brings me directly to my second point. It was important to me that the characters and their beliefs remained true to the prevailing worldview around the Zagros. Too often, authors project their own beliefs onto their characters. I aimed to create an authentic portrayal of how both the protagonists and antagonists, despite their vast differences, view the world. More important to me was that a reader might recognize themselves in those characters instead of feeling like they were reading a caricature of themselves.

Thirdly, I wanted to avoid this story being read as a political commentary. Make no mistake, it's impossible for an author to completely eliminate their political beliefs, but you can at least try not to let them take over the narrative. The story had to be set in a mythical past, a time and place that never existed, except in a shared imagination. This gave me the freedom to incorporate historical facts as I saw fit. For instance, the use of terms like princess and king refers to a form of governance that isn't necessarily common in Kurdish history. I also made a conscious effort to avoid naming modern states as much as possible.

Many will quickly recognize the stories of the Shahanameh. The Shahnameh is a Persian mythical narrative of Iran's history from the tenth century. And they will also recognize that I have taken many liberties in my story. For example, in the Shahnameh, Zahhak is imprisoned in Damavand rather than killed, a change that the conversation between Kawa and Runak alludes to. Additionally, in the original, Fereydun plays a much more significant role than in my story.

Those acquainted with myths in the region will understand that reinterpreting stories is a long-standing practice. For example, Zahhak predates the Shahnamah and can even be found in the Avesta, one of Zoroastrianism's holy books, from the fourth century. There, Zahhak is known as Azhi Dahaka and is more of a dragon than a man. And not only does the story extend further back in time, but it also reaches beyond present-day state borders. The term Azdaha can even be found in Pakistan, referring to a dragon.

The same applies to terms like peri, dew, and so on. I won't delve into them further here, as there are many references in this story that are deliberately left unexplained. They are there for the reader as an invitation for the reader to search further and to discover these ancient tales for themselves.

This book would not have been possible in its current form without the many people who have researched the Kurds, ancient stories, and translators. It would not have been possible without my editors Sabine Mourits and Kim Linssen, and Dr. Thoreau Redcrow, who edited this English translation. It would not have been possible without the proofreaders Nike Verwoert, Soz Raouf, Azad Qazaz, Shiba Hussein, Birgül Özmen and Nawa Azizi. And it would not have been possible without the literature recommendations of Professor Martin van Bruinessen. It also would not have been possible without the amazing illustrations by Julian Brzozowski and the subsequent updates made by Saad Salim and his team at Whitespace. But of all these people, my dear friend Thieme Stap deserves a special mention. No one has put in more unpaid hours than he. With sharp commentary and feedback, he contributed to elevating this work to a higher literary level. For this, he has my immense gratitude.

In many ways, this is a work of tragedy. The catalyst of the writing process was loss, and although it is about Kurds, I could not write it in Kurdish. It is a strange feeling to seek your origins and stumble upon an impenetrable language barrier. The barrier that the parents of us diaspora children had to overcome now confronts us in reverse.

But from tragedy springs beauty, and loss opens the door to a new self. I hope that this story can serve as a lasting testament to that truth.

www.ingramcontent.com/pod-product-compliance
Lightning Source LLC
LaVergne TN
LVHW090518110826
845146LV00003B/902

* 9 7 9 8 9 0 1 4 8 5 7 6 7 *